PAYMENT DEFERRED

C. S. FORESTER

Marble's only apparent way of getting out of debt is to poison his rich nephew and bury him in the garden. The subsequent course of his life is dictated by his obsessive fear of discovery.

Listed among the '99 Best Crime Stories' by the *Sunday Times*.

UNIFORM WITH THIS EDITION

Brown on Resolution

Death to the French

The Gun

ALSO PUBLISHED
BY THE BODLEY HEAD

Plain Murder

PAYMENT DEFERRED

C. S. FORESTER

THE BODLEY HEAD

LONDON SYDNEY
TORONTO

SBN 370 00657 7

Made and printed in Great Britain for
THE BODLEY HEAD LTD
9 Bow Street, London w.c.2
by William Clowes and Sons, Limited,
London and Beccles
Set in Linotype Baskerville
First published 1926
This edition 1959
Second impression 1968

CHAPTER I

'BE quiet children,' said Mrs Marble. 'Can't you see that father's busy?'

So he was. He propped his aching forehead on his hand, and tugged at his reddish moustache in an unhappy attempt at concentration. It was difficult to keep thinking about these wretched figures all the time, and it would have been even if Winnie did not try to poke John with a ruler in the intervals of squirming and muttering over her geometry homework. Mr Marble worried at his moustache while he peered at the column of figures on the scrap of paper before him. They seemed to be dancing in a faint mist under his eyes. He had been nerving himself for this effort for weeks now, and the instant that he began it he wanted to leave off. He was sure that looking at these figures would do no good. Nothing could do any good now.

The column of figures was headed briefly, 'Debts'. Rent was three weeks overdue, and that was the smallest item entered. He owed over four pounds each to the butcher and the baker, and the milk bill came to over five. How on earth had Annie managed to run up a five pound milk bill? He owed Evans, the grocer, more than six pounds. Mr Marble felt that he hated Evans, and had hated him ever since the time, a dozen years ago now, when they had arrived in Malcolm Road as a young couple, and Evans, apron, basket and whiskers complete, had called to solicit for their custom. Annie had just told him that Evans had

5

threatened to put the brokers in if he were not paid. The Bank would sack him for certain if anything like that happened. To Mr Marble's strained eyes the shape of Mr Evans suddenly seemed to loom over the paper he was regarding, with a flash of teeth and a leer in his eye like the devil he was. Mr Marble bit deep into the end of his pencil in a sudden flood of hatred.

There were some other items in the column too. The names of some of the men at the Bank appeared on the sheet of paper, and against them were set the amounts that Mr Marble owed them. Some of these men had even smaller incomes than his, and yet they managed nevertheless to keep out of debt—and even were sometimes able to lend money to poor devils like himself. But of course they weren't married, or if they were they did not have extravagant wives like Annie. Not that Annie was extravagant, though. Not really. She was just careless. Rather like himself, thought Mr Marble, with weary self-reproach, bending again to the figures. His debts amounted to no less than thirty pounds! On the asset side he had put nothing. He knew the amount of his assets too well to bother to do that. He was acutely aware of it. The balance in his account at the Bank was down to five shillings, and he had two florins in his pocket. There was no possibility of overdrawing. That would mean dismissal just the same.

It was his fault, he supposed weakly. He had seen this coming as long ago as last summer, and he had decided then that if they did without a holiday and spent nothing at Christmas they could get straight again. But they had had their holiday, and they had spent more than they should have done at Christmas. No, that had been Annie's fault. She had said that people would think it funny if they did not go to Worthing as she had told them they were going to do. And she had said it so often that in the end they had gone. And of course she had really been the cause of all those figures that were set against the names of men in the Bank on Mr Marble's little list. A man had to have a drink occasionally, when he slipped out of the office at half-past eleven, and of course he had to stand his friends one too, if they were with him. He could have paid for them easily if Annie had not spent all his money for him. And he had to smoke too, and have a good lunch occasionally. Mr Marble resolutely refused to think of how much he had spent on his hobby of photography. He knew that it was more than he should have done, and somewhere inside his conscience there was a nasty feeling that there was another bill, unreckoned in his list, due to the chemist at the end of the road for things he had bought for this purpose. The shelves in the bathroom upstairs were full of materials, and Mr Marble did not like to think of this, for he had never used half of them, having lately found more amusement in contemplating his hobby and buying things for it than in actually doing anything.

It was all very annoying and exasperating. How his head ached, and how tired he felt! His mind was numb. The grim feeling of blank despair was swamped by complete lassitude of soul. He realized vaguely that his oft-repeated threat of sending the children to bed without any supper would soon be carried into effect despite himself. He would be sacked from the Bank, and he would never get another job. He knew that well enough. He supposed it would end like the cases one read about in the paper, with his children's throats cut and himself and his wife dead of gas-poisoning. But at present he hardly cared. He wanted to relax. When those blessed kids had been packed off to bed he would drag the armchair up to the fire and put his feet up on the coalbox and read the paper and be comfortable for a bit. In the decanter in the sideboard there was a little drop of whisky left. Not much of course; three drinks perhaps, or maybe four. Mr Marble hoped it was four. With a drink and a paper and the fire he could forget his troubles for a little, for he couldn't do anything towards remedying them this evening. Mr Marble hardly realized that he had said the same thing to himself every evening for months now. The prospect seemed ineffably alluring. He yearned towards the decanter in the sideboard. And the wind was shrieking outside, sending the rain spattering against the windows. That would make it seem even more comfortable when he was beside the fire.

But the children must be disposed of first. For some obscure reason Mr Marble had an objection to drinking whisky in front of his children. His wife did not matter so much, although he would have preferred to have her out of the way too. A glance at the clock disappointed him a little. It was only half-past seven, and the children would not be going to bed for another half-hour at the earliest. He felt suddenly irritable. He peered surreptitiously from under his eyebrows to see if he could catch them misbehaving so as to send them off at once. The whisky would taste all the better if he could come to it fresh from a parental triumph and an autocratic exertion of authority.

'Stop that noise, John,' he ordered, with queer, feeble savageness.

John looked round from his chair by the fire a little startled. Five seconds ago he had been mazed in the pages of *How England saved Europe*, and had been leading the Fusilier Brigade over heaps of dead up the blood-stained hill of Albuera. He gazed vacantly at his father.

'Don't look at me like a fool,' spluttered Mr Marble. 'Do what you're told and stop that noise.' The two orders were synonymous, but John did not realize that.

'What did you tell me?' he asked vaguely.

'No impertinence, now. I said stop that noise.'

'What noise, father?' asked John, more to gain time to

8

collect his thoughts than for any other reason. But the question was fatal.

'Don't try to deny it,' said Mr Marble.

'Now, you were making a noise, you know, Johnny,' said Mrs Marble.

'You were kicking with your feet,' chimed in Winnie.

'I didn't deny it,' protested John.

'You did,' said Mrs Marble.

'You did,' said Winnie.

'Be quiet, Winnie,' snapped Mr Marble, rounding on his usual favourite in unusual fashion. 'You're as bad as he is, and you know it. Have you done your homework yet? I send you to a good school, and this is all the return I get for it.'

'Why, I got a scholarship,' replied Winnie, with a jerk of her head.

'Are you being impertinent too?' demanded Mr Marble. 'I don't know what you children are coming to. It's time for bed when you start being rude to your parents.'

The fatal words were said, and the children looked at each other in dismay. Mrs Marble made a typical faint-hearted effort on their behalf.

'Oh, not just yet, father,' she said.

That was all the opposition that Mr Marble needed to make him quite decided on the matter.

'At once,' he said. 'John, go to bed—and leave that book down here too. Winnie, pack your things neatly ready for the morning and go along too. Let this be a lesson to you.'

'But I haven't done my homework,' wailed Winnie, 'and there'll be such a row if I haven't done it to-morrow.'

John did not answer. He was wondering how the Fusiliers would get on without him for the rest of their advance. Even Mrs Marble was moved to further protest at this drastic action, but her half-hearted entreaties were ignored by both sides.

'Be quick, I am waiting,' said Mr Marble.

It was inevitable. Sullenly Winnie began to stack her books together. John stood up and put *How England saved Europe* on the table. It was then, at the eleventh hour, that diversion came. It came in the form of a loud knocking at the street door. For a second everyone looked at each other startled, for visitors were a rarity in Malcolm Road, especially at the extraordinary hour of half-past seven. Winnie recovered first.

'I'll go,' she said, and slipped through into the hall.

The others heard her tugging at the latch, and then the gas suddenly flickered as a gust of wind came rushing in with the opening of the street door. A strange, loud, masculine voice made itself heard asking for Mr Marble. He was about to go out too when Winnie reappeared.

'Somebody for you, father,' she said, and even as she spoke the owner of the strange voice came in behind her.

He was tall, and young, and seemed to be a study in browns, for he wore a brown trench coat and muffler, a brown tweed suit underneath, with brown shoes and socks. His face, too, was brown, although the shrieking wind outside had whipped it to a warm flush. He was young and debonair and handsome, and the sparkle of the raindrops on his muffler and the flash of his dark eyes and the gust of cold wind that entered the room at the same time as himself all combined to make his unexpected appearance as dramatic as even John, standing amazed by the fire, could wish for.

The stranger paused for a moment at the doorway.

'Good evening,' he said, a little diffidently.

'Good evening,' replied Mr Marble, wondering who on earth he was.

'I suppose you are my Uncle William,' said the new arrival. 'I didn't expect you to know me.'

'I'm afraid I don't.'

'My mother was Mrs Medland, Mrs Winnie Medland, your sister, sir, I think. I have just come from Melbourne.'

'Oh, of course. You're Winnie's boy? Come on in—no, let's get your coat off first. Annie, poke up the fire. Winnie, clear that stuff off that chair.'

Mr Marble bustled out into the hall with his guest. His family heard him helping him off with his coat, and then—

'And how is your mother now?'

There was no immediate answer to this question. The trench coat and the hat had been hung up on the hall-stand and the pair were about to reappear in the dining-room before the listeners there heard the hesitant, almost whispered, reply.

'She's dead. She died—six months ago.'

Mr Marble was still muttering the conventional condolences as they re-entered the dining-room, but he changed to clumsy brightness at the earliest possible moment. Truth to tell, he was not particularly interested in his sister Winnie, of whom he probably had not thought for the thirteen and a half years that had elapsed since he had had his daughter christened after her. Also he was feeling a little annoyed with this young man for turning up and interfering with the comfort of his evening. But Mr Marble was not the man to show it. Hostility of any kind—even the instinctive hostility towards strangers—was a feeling to be carefully concealed on every occasion. That was the lesson learned as a result of a lifetime spent in carrying out the orders of other people.

'Annie,' said Mr Marble, 'this is our young nephew, Jim. Do you remember him when he was a little boy, just going out to Australia with Winnie and Tom? I think I can. You wore a sailor suit, didn't you, er—Jim. Here, Winnie, this is a new cousin for you, one you never knew you had. Now sit down, sit down, man, and let's hear all your news.'

'Take that chair, Mr—Jim, I mean,' said Mrs Marble, stumbling in embarrassed fashion at having to address an opulently clothed and handsome stranger by his Christian name, 'you must be frozen.'

The new arrival was nearly as shy as was his hostess, but he suffered himself to be thrust into the best chair in the house—the one Mr Marble had coveted all the evening—while Mrs Marble ransacked her brain for something to talk about, and while the children drew as close as they could while remaining in the background.

Mr Marble plunged heavily into conversation.

'When did you arrive?' he asked.

'This morning only. I came on the *Malina,* arriving at Tilbury at twelve. In fact, I only reached London and found a hotel and had something to eat before coming here.'

'But how did you know we lived here?'

'Mother told me your address before she d-died.' The stumble was excusable. After all, the boy was no more than twenty. 'We'd often talked about this trip. She was coming with me, you see. She never liked Australia—I don't know why—and after father died—'

'Tom dead as well? That's bad luck.'

'Yes. He died the beginning of last year. It was that really that made mother—'

'Quite, quite,' Mrs Marble clucked in sympathetic chorus. She hated to hear of anyone dying.

Mr Marble made haste to change the conversation to matters more interesting.

'And how was your father's business getting on?' he demanded.

'Oh, pretty well. He made a lot of money during the war. He didn't want to, you know, but it just came, he said. But mother sold out after he died. She said she couldn't run that big shipping office by herself, and I was too young, and they offered a good price for it, so she took it.'

'So you're a young man of leisure now, eh?'

'I suppose so. I've only just come out of college, you know. Melbourne University. I'm having a look round to start with. That's what mother always planned for me.'

'Quite right too,' said Mr Marble, with the instinctive deference towards the independently rich which was by now an inevitable trait in his character.

For a moment the conversation flagged, and the boy, still a little shy, had leisure to look about him. These were the only relatives he had on earth, and he would like to make the most of them, although, he confessed to himself, he was not greatly attracted at first sight. The room was frankly hideous. The flowered wallpaper was covered with photographs and with the worst kind of engravings. The spurious marble mantelpiece was littered with horrible vases. Of the two armchairs one was covered with plush, the other with a chintz that blended unhappily with the wallpaper. The other chairs were plain bentwood ones. On a table in the window were dusty aspidistras in vast green china pots. In the armchair opposite him sat his uncle, in a shabby blue suit flagrantly spotted here and there. He was a small man, with sparse reddish hair and a bristling moustache of the same colour. His weak grey eyes bore a worried expression—more worried even than the expression he had already noticed in the eyes of the tired men who had sat opposite him in the bus which had brought him here. He had a silver watchchain across his rumpled waistcoat, and on his feet were shapeless carpet slippers, above which showed heather mixture socks sagging garterless round his ankles. Beside him, uncomplaining and uncomfortable on one of the bentwood chairs, sat his wife, frail, pale and shabby; the most noticeable thing about her was her lop-sided steel rimmed spectacles. The children were only visible to him when he turned his head uncomfortably. They certainly were more attractive. The little girl, Winnie, bore in her sharp features undeniable promise of good looks, as she sat with her hands in her lap beside the table, and the boy—John, wasn't he?—was quite a fair specimen of the fourteen-year-old. Nevertheless, young Medland did not feel at all at ease in his present situation. Six weeks on board a first-class liner, the only male passenger unmarried between the ages of fifteen and fifty is not the best introduction to the life of a poverty-stricken suburban home. Medland felt the sudden need to think about something else.

'May I smoke?' he asked.

'Why, yes, of course,' said Mr Marble, rousing himself suddenly to his hospitable duties.

Mr Marble plunged into his pocket in search of the battered yellow packet of cigarettes that lay there. It held three cigarettes he knew, and he had been treasuring them to smoke himself later in the evening. He spent as long as he could before producing them, and he was successful in his tactics. Medland already had produced his case and was offering it to him.

It was a leather case, the parting gift of one of the middle-aged women on the boat. Women never realize that a leather case spoils cigarettes. But this was far more than a cigarette case. It was a substantial wallet, with pockets for stamps and visiting cards, and at the back, sagging open in consequence of the way in which Medland held it, was a compartment for money. And this was full. Marble noticed, as the case was tendered to him, a thick fold of Treasury notes, twenty pounds at least, may be thirty, decided Marble, gauging it with a bank clerk's eye. Beside it was another fold of bank-notes— five pound notes, most probably. The sight positively dazzled poor Mr Marble's vision. And it brought, too, a ray of hope into the grim cells of dumb despair in his soul. It was more than flesh and blood could bear not to remark on it.

'That's a nice case,' said Mr Marble, tendering a lighted match to his guest.

'Yes.' Medland drew on his cigarette to make sure it was well lighted. 'It was a present,' he added modestly, and he held it out so that his uncle could see it more freely.

The bank-notes flashed once more before Marble's tortured eyes.

'Well lined too,' said Marble, striving to keep the envy out of his tone.

'Yes, I got them at Port Said—oh, you mean the notes?' Medland did his best not to show surprise at his uncle's bad taste. To assist in this he went into even further explanation. 'I had to cash one of my letters of credit as soon as I got to London. The voyage left me without a bean, pretty nearly, and what I had was Australian money, of course.'

It was an idle enough speech, but it sufficed to set Mr Marble thinking rapidly and unsteadily. This boy had arrived just in time to save him. He surely would not deny his new-found uncle a loan? Those Treasury notes would save him, let alone the bank-notes. And a loan from a nephew was not the same thing at all as a debt to that devil Evans, who would be putting the bailiffs in directly. It was not even in the same class as a debt to those men at the office, to repay whom only enough to keep them from complaining to higher officials had absorbed all his month's salary. On the heels of these thoughts came appalling realization of the peril of his position. It was the third of the month only, and he had ten shillings in the world with which to stave off his creditors and to support his family until his next pay-day. Before this he had shut his eyes to the position with all the small resolution he possessed. But now that there was a chance of escape the danger in which he stood was forced home upon him, making him shudder involuntarily a little and setting his heart thumping heavily in his chest. Mechanically he glanced across at the sideboard in which was the decanter. But he checked himself. He was not going to have to waste one of his last three—or was it four?—drinks on this boy. He thrust the thought of the whisky fiercely on one side and turned to making cautious advances towards the nephew.

'Did you have much difficulty in finding your way here?' he asked—the inevitable question always addressed to the newcomer to the suburbs.

'Oh, no,' replied Medland. 'I had your address, of course, mother dug it up from your old letters before she died. So I knew it was Dulwich, and in Trafalgar Square I saw dozens of buses all going to Dulwich, and I got on one and came as far as the terminus. Then it was easy. The first person I asked told me the way to Malcolm Road.'

'Just so. And where did you say you were staying?'

Medland had not said he was staying anywhere, but he told him. It was a substantial Strand hotel. It was then that Medland, apropos of this, made the remark that was to alter everything.

'It's funny to think of,' he said, striving to keep the conversation going, 'but besides you there isn't a soul in England who knows anything about me. I don't think I was in the hotel more than an hour, and I only left my hand luggage there. The rest of my stuff is at Euston. What with going to the Bank and so on I simply didn't have time to collect it, even if it had got there. I was thinking to myself as I came here that if I got lost and never found my way back no one would mind at all— except you, of course.'

'H'm!' said Mr Marble, and another train of thought came to him on the instant, and he shuddered again.

Medland's shyness was turning to boyish talkativeness. He looked round to the two children.

'Well,' he said, and smiled, 'you two don't seem to have much to say for yourselves.'

Winnie and John still remained silent. They had been keeping as quiet as mice so as not to draw attention to themselves and raise again the postponed question of bed. But beside this John was lost in admiration of this weather-tanned man who had come all the way from Australia, and who treated such an amazing trip through pirate-haunted seas with so little concern that he had said no word about it. And he spoke so casually about hotels too. John had noticed last year at Worthing that his father spoke of people who lived in hotels as opposed to those who live in rooms, and even in boarding-houses, with awe in his voice. And this man lived in a hotel and thought nothing of it!

As for Winnie, she was thinking that he was the most beautiful man she had ever seen. His warm brown face and his brown tweeds with their intoxicating scent were wonderful. Then when he looked straight at you and smiled, as he had just done, he was handsomer than anyone she could imagine, far handsomer than the fairy prince in the pantomime at Christmas.

'Speak up, children,' said their father. To Medland's fastidious ear it sounded as if he might have added, 'Tell the pretty gentleman his fortune.'

The children grinned shyly. Winnie could say nothing. But John made an effort, unused as he was to conversation owing to severe repression by his father during his queer moods of late.

'You have kangaroos in Australia, haven't you?' he said, with a fourteen-year-old wriggle.

'You're right,' said Medland. 'I've hunted them too.'

'Ooh,' gasped John ecstatically. 'On horseback?'

'Yes, for miles and miles across the country, as fast as your horse could gallop. I'll tell you about it some day.'

Both children writhed in delight.

'And bushrangers?' said John. 'Did—did you ever see Ned Kelly?'

To Medland's credit he did not laugh.

'No such luck,' he said. 'There weren't many round where I lived. But I know a topping book about them.'

'*Robbery under Arms*,' said both children at once.

'Oh, you've read it?'

'Read it? I should think they had.' This was Mr Marble's contribution to the conversation. 'They're terrors for reading, those two kids are. Never see 'em without a book.'

'That's fine,' said Medland.

But the conversation wilted beyond recovery at this intrusion. And Marble, intent on getting Medland to himself, flashed a look at the children and jerked his head skywards. They understood, and climbed down dolefully from their chairs.

'Bedtime, children?' said Mr Marble in a tone of surprise that was unsuccessful in its purpose of deceiving Medland, since he had caught the tail end of Marble's signal. 'Good night, then. Why, aren't you going to kiss me?'

They had not been intending to do so. The custom had died out months before, when Marble had begun turning to the decanter in the sideboard for distraction from his troubles, and with children a custom three months unused might as well never have existed. Besides, John was nearly too old for kissing now. Both John and Winnie kissed their father awkwardly, and their mother casually. Then John shook hands with his new cousin. It was the first time he had ever shaken hands as man to man, with eye meeting eye in man's fashion, and he was very proud of it. Winnie, too, tried to shake hands in imitation of her brother, but there was something in Medland's smile and in the gentle traction he exerted on her hand that made her lean forward and kiss the boyish mouth tendered to her. It felt funny, different from other kisses she had known. It was a very silent pair that went up to bed.

Marble turned away with evident relief as they closed the door.

'Now we can be comfortable,' he said. 'Draw your chair up closer to the fire, er—Jim. What a night,' he added, as the wind howled outside.

Medland nodded moodily. He was feeling awkward. He was not at all at home with these strange people. He didn't like the way Marble behaved towards his children. The kids were all right of course, and the mother was a nonentity. But there was an atmosphere about the place that he hated. He pulled himself together and tried to shake off the brooding premonitory mood that was oppressing him. It was absurd, of course. Old Marble was only a very ordinary sort of chap. Seedy and down at heel, but quite all right. He was smiling oilily at present, but that didn't mean anything necessarily. Hang it all, if he didn't like the place he could clear out in a few minutes' time and never come back to it. For the matter of that Medland's thoughts swerved suddenly to the utterly absurd—he could change his hotel next morning and then they could never find him again. The bare idea was sufficient to bring his mind back to reality. There was no reason why he should think about things like that at all. The kids were fine, and he'd see a lot of them while he was in England. He could take them to a lot of the places he felt he had to go to, the Tower of London and St Paul's, for instance. That would be topping.

Mr Marble was speaking to his wife.

'What about some supper, Annie?' he was saying. 'I expect our young friend here is hungry.'

'But—' began Mrs Marble hopelessly, and then checked herself hastily and clumsily as she caught sight of her husband frowning at her.

'Don't worry about me, please,' put in Medland. 'I dined just before I came out.'

'That's all right, then,' replied Marble. 'I dined just after I came in.'

And he laughed. The laughter was just the least bit strained.

Conversation began again, resuming its hopeless, desultory way while Medland wondered in a bored, young man's fashion why on earth he did not get up and go at once. There were really several reasons. One was that the wind and the rain were continually making themselves heard outside; another was that the fire was most attractive—it was the most attractive thing in the whole house —but deep down there was a feeling of relief that he was not in a hotel with nothing special to do. Medland had laid plans for a very exciting time on his arrival in England, but at the moment he was feeling a little homesick and not in the mood for excitement of any kind. It might have been as well if he had felt otherwise.

Mrs Marble came into the picture at times. She asked him homely questions as to whether he was sea-sick on the voyage, and whether he had enough to eat, and whether he was warmly enough clad to face an English winter. Medland answered politely enough, but Marble was positively rude to her on more than one occasion. Medland found himself regarding the little man curiously. His face was a little moist, and his eyes were brighter than they had been before, as though he was growing excited about something of which the others knew nothing. He cut his wife short repeatedly, and his questions grew more and more personal. Medland realized that to a person of Marble's character the idea of conversation would consist of a series of questions, but even that was no excuse for this searching cross-examination as to his resources, his friends and his knowledge of affairs.

Poor Marble! And poor Medland! Marble was being affected more and more by the realization of his position, rendered more acute by envious contrast with Medland's, while Medland's every answer seemed calculated to urge Marble on to—something. Marble was not quite sure what it was. It could not just be borrowing money; he had decided to attempt that hours ago. The thumping heart within him seemed to indicate something more unusual than that. Marble was nerving himself to definite action— for the first time in his life, be it added.

With the cunning of the weak, he did his best to disguise the state he was in, while all the time, without conscious volition on his part, his furtive mind was twisting and turning, devising the course of action he was likely to take. No wonder Medland looked at him oddly at times.

Time seemed to be passing with extraordinary rapidity. It seemed to Marble that every time he looked at the clock on the mantelpiece another half-hour had fled. Twice had he detected in Medland's manner an intention of leaving as soon as the conversation broke, and each time he had flung himself into the breach, talking nonsense, as he was painfully aware, in order to stave off the crisis that would arise when that time came.

His fevered mind roused itself to additional activity. He nerved himself to make the sacrifice which he realized was inevitable, and gathered himself together in his chair as casually as he could manage.

'What about a drink?' he asked. In such a matter-of-fact way did he bring the question out that Medland did not guess the wrench it cost him.

Medland hesitated before he replied; he was not yet a

man of the world enough to regard an offer of a drink as an ordinary event; and during that little hesitation Marble had risen and walked across to the sideboard, beyond the table. For a moment he was lost to view as he dived down below the level of the table; when he rose again he had a siphon of soda-water—half full—under his arm, two tumblers in one hand, and in the other, held very carefully, a decanter of whisky, a quarter full. He set these things out on the table near his chair; he was standing very close to his wife as he did so. He took the opportunity of mumbling something to her. He spoke swiftly and obscurely, so obscurely that Medland, though he noticed the act, could not hear the words, and took them to be some hint as to domestic arrangements—probably a comment on the shortage of whisky. What Marble had really said was: 'Want talk business. Go to bed. Say headache.'

Annie Marble heard the words some time before she attached any meaning to them. That was usual with her. Even when she realized their significance, slight enough to her, she did not act at once upon them. It was always a long time before she could co-ordinate her faculties to change from one course of action to another.

Marble poured out a drink with great deliberation. It was not a very generous one, for he was confronted with the problem of offering his guest as much as possible while conserving for himself enough at least to keep up appearances; yet his whole soul was crying out for that whisky. His hand shook a little as he poured, so that the decanter chattered faintly on the rim of the tumbler, but he took a firm grasp of his nerves with a last despairing effort and completed the business, without having consulted his guest as to quantity even to the usual conventional extent. Then he sat back in his chair, half in anguish, half in satisfaction. He had managed the pouring out perfectly, he told himself. He had given Medland

plenty while quite a respectable amount remained in the
decanter. Easily enough for two more drinks, anyway, and
the half-formed plot in Marble's mind demanded that
there should be enough for two drinks left in the decanter. But it was a frightful effort for him to sip casually
from the cool tumbler in his hand. He wanted that drink
so terribly badly, but all he could allow himself to do
was to nod perfunctorily across to Medland, sip just a
little, and then put the glass down indifferently beside
him. But even that small amount was enough to calm
his shrieking nerves, so that his shaking body became as
calm and detached as his scheming, uncontrolled mind.

As he replaced the glass Annie Marble rose. She knew
the role it was necessary for her to assume, and by some
strange freak of mental poise she did it perfectly. Her
dim mind had never fully realized the grim peril in which
lay the fortunes of her husband and herself; nothing that
Marble could say—and he said little—would force it
home to her as long as she could go on obtaining credit
at the shops; but she knew they were in some trouble, and
that Marble was intending that this young nephew of his
should help them out. It behoved her therefore to do her
best, quite apart from the fact that her negative personality responded in small actions to every whim of her
husband, just as he wished.

'I think I shall go to bed, Will,' she said rising a little
wearily from the uncomfortable bentwood chair. 'I've got
a bit of a headache.'

Mr Marble was greatly concerned.

'Really, dear?' he said, rising. 'That's bad luck. Have
a nightcap before you go up?' And he nodded towards
the decanter.

But even as he nodded, with his face away from Medland, there was a little scowl between his eyebrows that
gave Mrs Marble her cue.

'No, dear, thank you,' she said, 'I'll just go straight up and it will be better in the morning.'

'Just as you like,' said Mr Marble.

Mrs Marble moved across to Medland.

'Good night, er—Jim,' she said, shaking hands.

'Good night. I hope it will really be better to-morrow.'

'Good night, dear,' said Mr Marble, 'I won't disturb you when I come up if I can help it. I expect I shall be a bit late.'

He pecked her on her cold cheek—a typical marital kiss. But Mr Marble was not in the habit of kissing his wife good night at all, and he never worried in the least about disturbing her when he came to bed. However, it gave the scene that calm domestic atmosphere that Mr Marble's subconscious mind, which had him in full control, had decided was necessary to the occasion.

Mrs Marble had gone, and they heard the dragging steps on the floor of the room above.

'No need for hurry, I suppose, seeing that you're a gay young bachelor,' said Mr Marble.

'None at all,' replied Medland, and regretted saying it the instant it was said. He had really no desire to go on being bored for a further interminable period. But his answer had committed him to another half-hour at the very least, and he endeavoured to reconcile himself to it.

Just for a brief space Mr Marble regained full control over himself, and he made a brief and unavailing struggle against the inevitable which a stronger power within him was forcing upon him. He began to talk again on the subject of Medland's money—the subject on which his lack of decent reticence had already annoyed his guest.

'So you're quite a well-off young man now, it seems?' he said, with exasperating joviality.

'I suppose so,' was the curt reply.

'A good bit to spare for investments, I suppose?'

It was a blundering way of putting it, and it failed.

24

Even on the voyage over more than one man had come to Medland with get-rich-quick schemes, and he had contrived to see through them. And so many people had borrowed money from him that the process was both familiar and annoying to him. Medland determined to stop this attempt once and for all. It might be awkward for a bit, but it would save endless trouble in the future. He looked straight into Marble's eyes.

'No,' he said, 'I haven't any to invest. I'm quite satisfied with the arrangement that my father made before he died. I've got just enough, and no more. And I put up with it.'

That settled the matter definitely enough for anyone, but, to Medland's surprise, Marble showed no sign of discomfiture. Medland did not know it, but at a bound the lurking power within his uncle had regained possession of him, and had at once begun to smooth the way for the inevitable.

'A good thing too,' said Marble, and his manner of saying it left Medland seriously in doubt as to whether his former question had really been a feeler for a loan. 'The market's in a rotten state at present. I shouldn't like to buy at all just now, not gilt-edged. Sit tight and hang on to what you've got, that's my motto all the time nowadays.'

He said it in all sincerity, and Medland actually felt himself warming towards him. At that time Medland was in serious danger of falling into the delusion that so often attacks men of wealth who have had their wealth from boyhood and have been 'stung' too often by the unscrupulous—he was in danger of imagining that everyone with whom he came into contact was seeking profit at his expense. The surest way to his heart was to convince him of the contrary, and that Mr Marble, in those few instants, had nearly succeeded in doing.

The conversation swung easily into discussion of the

investment market, and that without the personal note that Medland so much resented. Somewhere within him Marble possessed a clever turn for finance, which hitherto he had been unable, as well as too lazy, to exert. Medland, with a hard head for business inherited from his ship-broking father, recognized a surprisingly kindred spirit. For the first time that evening he really began to enjoy himself. He drained his glass almost without thinking of it—enthusiasm succeeded in overcoming his juvenile distaste for whisky even though he had never been able to make himself like it.

Marble was watching him with fierce intentness through narrowed eyes. Medland hardly noticed it, and attached no importance to it if he did. Then Marble pulled himself out of his chair, glass in hand, and addressed himself to the decanter. That foolish heart of his was thumping again, thumping heavily, but it did not affect his actions. They were quite under control—the control of that inward force which had taken charge of him and which recognized the inevitable.

Marble reached across and drew Medland's glass from his hand. 'There's only one more drink apiece,' said Marble. 'I'm sorry, but we weren't expecting visitors to-night, you know.'

He said it in such a matter-of-fact way that Medland had no chance even of trying to refuse the second drink. Idly Medland watched Marble pour out the whisky from the decanter with the painful care that had characterized his action before. The liquid stood level in the two tumblers. Marble was apparently about to splash in the rest of the soda-water from the siphon when he paused as though listening.

'Just a minute,' he said, 'I think one of the kids is calling out.'

Medland had heard nothing, but he was unused to the noises of the house and made no question. Mr Marble had heard nothing, either. He had said what he did as an excuse to withdraw from the room and go upstairs. It was the most natural action in the world for him to creep out of the room to listen to hear if either of his children was frightened, and it was most natural too, that he should be carrying in his hand the tumbler that he had held at the moment his attention was distracted. Medland watched him go; everything was so natural that he did not give a second thought to it.

Hardly more than a minute later Marble came tiptoeing back down the stairs and into the room, the glass still in his hand.

'False alarm,' he said. 'One gets used to these things when one is the father of a family.'

He turned again to the siphon, and it hissed into the tumblers. Then he passed Medland's across to him. As he took it the wind outside howled again louder than ever; the windows rattled and they heard the rain pelting against the glass.

'What a night,' said Medland.

'Drink up,' replied Marble, very, very calmly.

CHAPTER II

WHEN Annie Marble woke in the early morning she was oppressed with a headache—a real headache, this time. She had had a restless night, although, true to his word, astonishingly enough, her husband had not disturbed her when he came up. At this very moment he was sleeping heavily at her side. She turned in the bed and looked at him in the half light that was straying through the untidy blinds. He lay on his back, his sparse hair standing on end, his eyes closed and his mouth open, his bristling red moustaches reinforced now by a coarse but scanty growth of beard. His hands clutched the sheets, and his breath passed in and out of his mouth with a stertorous sound. To most people he would have been an unpleasing picture, but Annie Marble did not think so. She was used to it in any case, and his present helpless attitude and appearance always roused the mother spirit within her which was almost her sole ordinary characteristic now. She would have liked to have taken him into her arms and hugged him a little, but she would not do so for fear of disturbing him.

Instead, she began to wonder whether he had been successful in his management of his interview with the strange nephew last night. She hoped so. She knew he had been worried about money lately; he had told her so on occasions. And he had cut down the money he was accustomed to give her. That didn't matter much, as Mr Evans and the milkman and the others were all so obliging. But he had been bothered about it, she knew. So she hoped the nephew—she was sure she would never learn to call such a splendid young man plain 'Jim'—had done something for them. He ought to have done, for he had stayed long enough. She had heard them talking long after she had settled herself to sleep. The remembrance brought a new rush of dim recollections to her mind. Will had come upstairs then, just when she was nearly asleep. She remembered wondering what he came for. He had gone into the bathroom; she had heard his keys rattle as he unlocked, she supposed, his photographic cupboard. It was probably to get something he wanted to show Jim. There, she had got it quite natural that time. Jim must be interested in photography too.

For a space her muddled thoughts followed no settled line. Then she came back to last night. If Jim was interested in photography he must have done something for Will—to Annie's mind everything was done for everybody by somebody else. And she must have been dreaming when she thought she heard that loud cry. She was awake just afterwards, she knew; she must have been dreaming that someone had called out loud, and had awakened still dreaming it. Yes, that must have been it, and she must have gone to sleep again and started dreaming again at once, for she had a hazy, muddled recollection of hearing a strange noise downstairs, as though something was being dragged along the linoleum of the passage downstairs, and one or two sharp taps as though some things were dropping sharply from one step to another on the little dark staircase just outside the kitchen door. What a silly thing to dream!

So Jim must have done something for Will. That was a good thing. She hoped Will would tell her all about it when he had the chance, because generally he did not tell her anything, and she was not much good at guessing. It was a little bit of a pity that Will said so little, for he could talk so nicely when he was in the mood. But, there, you can't have everything. And Will was *such* a dear all the time. And just now he looked such a baby, such a nice little baby. She did wish she could take him in her arms just for a moment or two, the way she used to hold John, and Winnie too, when they were little. They weren't such babies now, and tried to get on without their mother, and she felt a little bit lonely sometimes. When Will wasn't worried by things she could still love him like that, though. It was a pity that he was worried such a lot nowadays. But now that Jim had done something for him it would be all right perhaps. She would buy some new nightdresses, like those in the windows in Rye Lane, very warm and nice, but looking quite nice, too, with

nearly real lace on the edges of the sleeves. Then perhaps
—but here the alarum on the table at her side went off,
and she had to stop thinking.

The sudden noise brought her husband to a sitting-up
position in an instant. He was still grasping the sheets,
and his erect hair made him look so like a frightened baby
that Mrs Marble laughed. He glared and blinked at her
uncomprehendingly for a while.

'W—what is it?' he demanded.

To Mrs Marble, mentally constituted as she was, no
strange mood came amiss, or seemed strange to her.

'It's just the clock, dear,' she said, 'half-past seven.'

'The clock?' said Mr Marble. 'I thought—I was dreaming. Just the clock?'

He still muttered to himself as he snuggled down into
the bed again, with his face hidden by the pillows. Annie
had never known him mutter to himself before, but he
was still muttering and mumbling to himself as she began
to dress. Then suddenly he stopped muttering, and sat
upright again in the bed.

'By God!' he said. 'I wasn't dreaming.'

He threw off the bedclothes and climbed stiffly out of
the bed. He looked like a pathetic little boy in his striped
blue and white pyjamas as he hobbled across the room,
to where his clothes were piled untidily on a chair. He
tumbled some of these on the floor as he seized his coat,
and he plunged his hand into the breast-pocket. Annie
could not see what he found there, but apparently it
confirmed his suspicions. He stared vacantly across the
room for several seconds, the coat dangling from his
hands.

'No,' he repeated, 'I wasn't dreaming.'

He hobbled stiffly but feverishly back across the room
and thrust his feet into his carpet slippers, and then hurried out of the room. Annie, amazed, heard him enter
Winnie's bedroom next door. Then she heard him pull

up the blind there, while Winnie sleepily inquired what was the matter, unanswered. Annie simply did not understand it. It was the first time she could ever remember his getting out of bed before breakfast was ready. But she could not wait to reflect on the matter. She huddled on the rest of her clothes and hastened downstairs to look after breakfast.

There was no end to the surprises of that day. To begin with, Mr Marble came down in his Sunday clothes of neat blue serge, instead of the dilapidated suit which he usually wore to business, and he only replied to Annie's innocent and inevitable remark on this strange phenomenon with a scowl. He had not come straight down into the dining-room, as was his wont, either. Instead, he had gone into the tiny and seldom entered sitting-room at the back, and Annie, hastening in duty bound to see what he wanted, found him staring out of the window at the little patch of muddy backyard beyond. It was the same view as he must have seen when he went so surprisingly into Winnie's bedroom. He could see it at any time when he was home, and he must have seen it several hundred, but for all that he was peering through the window at the muddy bed, flowerless as ever, with an intentness that even Annie noticed. It was extraordinary. It was true that by getting up as soon as she had done he was a quarter of an hour ahead of his usual time, yet even that was no reason for his wasting a good five minutes after his breakfast out in the yard wandering aimlessly up and down as though he was looking for something. Yet even Annie could see that he was relieved not to find anything.

During breakfast there was nothing unusual. Mr Marble ate little, but that was his way, and he said less, but no one ever said anything at breakfast at 53 Malcolm Road. John was deep in homework he had to prepare for school, and Winnie sewed a button on her glove in the interval of eating porridge. But after breakfast, while

Mrs Marble was in the passage with her husband helping him on with his coat, he pulled from his pocket, loose, as though he had laid them there ready, a small roll of Treasury notes.

'Here,' he said, 'take these, and for God's sake go and pay Evans off this morning. And we aren't going to deal with him any more. Get what you want from Richards' in the future. There's enough there for Evans' bill and a bit over.'

Annie took the notes thankfully.

'Oh, I am so glad, dear,' she said. 'So Jim did do something for you after all?'

'Eh?' said Mr Marble suddenly, and she shrank back as she caught sight of the expression on his face. 'What do you mean?' he said.

'Nothing, dear, except that. Why—what——?'

But Mr Marble had snatched open the door and was striding off. He was muttering again.

Truly, Annie had much to think about as she began her daily household duties, and even she felt what a pity it was that she could not think very clearly. There was Will's stiffness, now. He was so stiff that he could hardly walk that morning, and she had never known that since before they were married and he used to play football. But Will couldn't have been playing football last night, could he now? It made her anxious. Then upstairs a new surprise awaited her. Will's other suit, his old everyday one, lay in a tumbled heap on the bedroom floor. She picked it up and put it away. It was sopping wet, and it was thick with mud. That must be why he did not wear it in the morning. How could he have got it so wet and muddy? The idea of football came to her mind again, but of course that was silly. Will did not play football now, and if he did it wouldn't be late at night and in his ordinary clothes. With a sigh she left the problem alone and went on tidying the room. Then there were

Winnie's and John's bedrooms to be done, and after that a look round just to see that everything was in order. In the bathroom an old memory recurred to her. Will had come in here last night. Perhaps she could see what he came for? But she could see nothing different from usual as she looked round. The locked, glass-fronted cupboard in which Will kept his chemicals hung on the wall beside her. She peered in, as she had done hundreds of times before. The manifold bottles meant nothing to her; but she liked to look at the labels and wonder what they were all about. Some of the bottles were of a mysterious brown, and some were white. They were all very neatly arranged. Except one, and that was a little out of its place on the shelf. (As it might be if a man had put it back there in the dark.) Annie glanced casually at the label. It conveyed nothing to her at all, but it happened that the queer name stuck in her mind—potassium cyanide. She turned away from the cupboard without further thought.

There was a pleasurable little excursion before her. She felt quite thrilled with imagining it as she put on her hat before her bedroom mirror. It was a long time since she had had a lot of money in her pocket as she had now. Not that it would stay there long, as she had to pay off Evans' bill, but it made her feel very rich and great to go into Evans' shop and ask, in quite a matter-of-fact way, for her bill, and then to open her bag and produce a roll of notes and hand over the amount as if she were accustomed to such transactions every minute of her life. That would be nice, and then she would go on to Richards', and walk in there, and Mr Richards would be so nice to her because she was a new customer, and she would order what she wanted, and he would say 'Yes, madam', and 'No, madam', as if her every word was law. She was glad that Jim had done something for Will. Otherwise she would not be having such a happy day.

After all, by contrast with the ordinary day of a woman with a house to look after, it would be a happy day.

She was still feeling happy when Mr Marble returned from the office in the evening, just after the children had had their tea and were settling down to their homework. He looked very tired, poor soul, and he still walked stiffly, but Mrs Marble had a nice tea ready for him thanks to her visit to Mr Richards' shop. There were nice scrambled eggs, good eggs, not the other kind, and three pieces of toast, and there was fresh tea in the pot. Mrs Marble was disappointed when he looked at the pleasant tea-table with evident distaste. He flung himself down in an arm-chair with a sigh.

'Anybody been?' he demanded.

'No, dear, no one,' replied Annie, surprised.

'Sure?'

'Of course I am, dear. Who is there to come? There was no one besides the milkman, and people selling things. It wasn't Mr Brown's day for the insurance.'

'That's all right then,' said Mr Marble, and he began to unwrap the parcel he had brought in with him. The children looked up with interest, but they were disappointed. It was only a stupid old bottle of whisky. But Mr Marble loked at it very eagerly.

'Aren't you going to have your tea, dear?' asked Mrs Marble.

Mr Marble looked, hesitated, and looked again.

'Oh, all right, then,' he said grudgingly.

He sat down before his tray and began to eat while his wife began her delightful duty of looking after him, pouring out his tea, refilling the teapot from the kettle on the fire, and seeing that he was comfortable. But Mr Marble had hardly begun when he rose from the table and hurried out of the room. Annie, hurt and mystified, heard him in the sitting-room next door—for the second time that day, and yet perhaps the second time for

34

months. Almost mechanically she followed him, to find him peering through the window in the half light out into the backyard, where there was a small rain falling. He started as he heard her behind him.

'What are you following me about for like this?' he snapped.

'Nothing dear. Is there anything you want, dear?'

'Nothing, dear. Anything you want, dear?' he gibed. 'Only a wife with some sense. That's all.'

He pushed past her without apology, back to the dining-room. She found him there seated at the table, but he had pushed his nice tray away, and was staring gloomily at the whisky bottle, which was perched, like some family god, in the exact centre of the table. He could not take his eyes off it. He did not look up as she came in, nor did he speak. For some minutes there was quiet in the room, broken only by the scratching of Winnie's pen and the whispering of the two children to themselves as they toiled over their homework. Annie ought to have taken away the tray and started the washing up. That was her next duty, but for some reason she did not do it. Mr Marble's gaze shifted from the whisky bottle, and fixed itself on the tablecloth. Clearly he was following some new train of thought. Suddenly he moved uneasily in his chair, and then he looked up.

'Has Mrs What's-her-name been here to-day?' he asked his wife. 'Oh, you know who I mean—the washerwoman person.'

'No, dear, of course not. She comes on every other Monday. She won't be coming until Monday week.'

'Well, she's not to come at all. You must do the washing yourself if you can't afford to send it out.'

'Of course we can't afford to send it out, dear. Laundries are dreadfully expensive now.'

'Then you must do it yourself.'

'But I don't want to. Why must I, Will? It's dreadfully hard work.'

'Hard work never killed anyone yet. I'm not going to have strange women in *my* house and hanging up clothes in *my* garden any more. That's why.'

'But——'

'That's enough, now. Do what I say and don't argue.' And Mr Marble turned his gloomy gaze once more to the whisky bottle.

Poor Annie was almost crying. It had been such a nice day up to now, and now everything was going wrong. To cover her whimpering sniffs she took up the tray and went with it down the stairs into the kitchen.

Mr Marble eyed the whisky bottle. He felt he needed some, despite the fact that he had already had three or four—or was it five or six?—whiskies that day. He was very tired, very, very tired, and his head ached. Just as it ached this time yesterday. No, he didn't want to think about yesterday. How his arms ached with that digging! He ought to have caught cold, too, seeing how it had been raining, but he hadn't. Pure Scotch Whisky. Very plain on the bottle, but it was good stuff inside. God, but it was! An indescribably passionate longing to drink came over him, and he scraped his chair back from the table and fetched the corkscrew from the sideboard drawer. He drew the cork rapidly and dexterously. Not a scrap fell into the bottle. Then he found himself a tumbler and stood it beside the bottle. There was no soda-water left after last night, but he didn't want soda-water. He didn't want anything besides the relief that he knew a few sips of that yellow liquid would bring him. He fingered the bottle lovingly, still standing by the table. Suddenly he became aware of his children's gaze upon him. Glad of the distraction from the drudgery of home-work, they had been sitting silently watching his every movement. With a gust of fury Marble realized that it was impossible for him to drink with those solemn eyes upon him. He put the bottle down again upon the table with a thump.

'Confound you kids!' he said furiously. 'Why on earth aren't you in bed?'

Neither child spoke. The doom was close upon them again, they knew, and this time it was more than could be hoped for for another new arrival to postpone it, as had happened so miraculously yesterday. But if they kept quiet and pretended to be closely occupied with their work it might be all aright. They buried their noses in their books. Marble could only see the tops of their heads, moving a little as they pored over their writing.

'Bah!' he said. 'Don't act about like that. Shut up those books and go to bed. At once, now.'

Under more favourable circumstances they would have protested that it was not nearly bedtime yet. They should have pointed out that it was only a little after seven o'clock, and they were entitled to another hour at least. But they knew, in the intuitive manner of children, that this time the less they said the better for them. They began silently to pack up their books.

'Go to bed! Go to bed!' raved Mr Marble.

'Don't look at me like that, sir,' thundered Mr Marble. He had suddenly become half hysterical with rage. He pounded on the table with the whisky bottle, crazy with thwarted eagerness. John turned his scowling face in another direction, but the expression on his face was unchanged, and served to drive his father more frantic than ever, if that were possible. He reached out and struck the boy a heavy blow with his open hand, making him stagger.

They went, without a word, but the scowl on John's face had somehow something triumphant about it now. If he was going to be sent to bed in arbitrary fashion, he would at least see that his father lost his temper during the process. John always felt he disliked his father during these queer moods of his—and the moods were becoming more and more frequent too.

The children went, and Mr Marble sighed with relief. He dragged his armchair up to the fire, and put the small table beside it for his glass. He would wait and be quite methodical now that a drink was an immediate certainty. He poured himself out a moderate drink and tossed it off. He felt better at once, more peaceful, more *safe*. He refilled his glass, and set it beside him. Then he sat down comfortably by the fire and gazed at the leaping flames. This was just what he wanted to do yesterday, before that wretched boy turned up and spoilt his evening. But it was even better than yesterday, because then he had only three drinks in the decanter. Now he had a whole bottle full, which would last him for this evening at least, without any thought of stinting. It was fine not having to stint. He wouldn't have to stint in any direction at all for another two weeks at least, thank goodness, or for a lot more than that, if only he were to change those five-pound notes. And after all, why shouldn't he? Of course the one-pound notes were as safe as anything, but the fivers ought to be just as safe too. They wouldn't give anything away, even if they were traced from Medland to himself. And if he took care and only cashed them at places where he wasn't known they wouldn't be traced at all. Anyway what did it all matter? It was silly to think that he was going to all the trouble he went to last night just to pay off a miserable thirty pounds of debts. Better to be hung for a sheep than for a lamb. Stop! Why was he thinking about hanging?

Mrs Marble, re-entering from the kitchen, saw her husband reach out greedily for the glass on the table at his side, and swallow its contents in violent gulps. Then she knew that dear Will would be unapproachable for the rest of the evening, and she would not be able to have that pleasant chat with him about what Jim had done for them that she had been looking forward to all day. Mrs Marble was rather disappointed.

CHAPTER III

YET for some weeks Mr Marble hesitated about changing those five-pound notes. He was of mixed character. When he had been a rat in a corner he had fought like one, desperately, to the last risk, but now he had escaped he thought of nothing except flight and covering his tracks.

And he was paying heavily enough for those few Treasury notes. That heart of his which had thumped so heavily on that stormy evening thumped just as heavily at other times now. He could not keep his mind from working out possible occurrences in the future, and some new morbid thought of the arrival of the police, instigated by the officials of Medland's hotel, or of some unexpected inquiry by the Bank as to whence had come the money which had so suddenly come into his possession, would set his heart pounding away until he could only lean back in his chair and gasp. He would wake sweating in the night too, with the fevered blood running hot under his skin, as some fantastic possibility developed in his sleeping mind. Then he would writhe and toss in his bed, muttering faintly to himself, tortured with fears of the known and of the unknown. And sometimes, when he had been sleeping very badly, one or two horrible memories returned to him: memories of a pair of staring eyes, and of a boyish face, the mouth smeared with foam. That was the worst of all.

He was not even happy sitting alone in the dining-room at Malcolm Road, with a full bottle of his only friend beside him, and calm in the knowledge that *no one was poking about in the garden*. The whisky only made him think the more at first. It took a long time before he could stop his mind from thinking about what might happen, and he soon found the worst moments of all were those at the beginning of the evening, when the whisky only bit and did not deaden. At times the prospect so frightened him that he flinched from his preliminary torture, and would go through the evening without drinking at all, although every fibre of his body seemed to be shrieking for it. These were the times when he craved for the company of his wife and children; when he would encourage Annie to long monologues about how she had spent her day. To Marble, sitting back in his chair, with Annie droning away beside him about her encounter with the baker's boy, who now worked for the butcher instead, and how she went down Rye Lane to buy remnants at the sale, and what Mr Brown, the insurance agent, had to say, it seemed incredible that anything unusual had happened. It must have all been a wild dream. If it were reality, how then could he be sitting at his fireside so peacefully? Brief monosyllables were sufficient to keep Annie talking and Mr Marble had ample time to think of all this. It was too like a fantastic nightmare for anything really to have happened in this very room, this poky, stuffy, suburban dining-room, and for a terrible secret to be hidden away in the garden just outside. Drugged by Annie's talk, or by John's or Winnie's chatter about school, Mr Marble not infrequently succeeded in persuading himself that it was indeed a dream. And Annie was so pleasantly fluttered and flattered by his attention in listening to her like this! But when night came, Mr

Marble paid for his relaxation. Then, on the verge of sleep, he would realize that it was not a dream—and he would spend the night turning and tossing in fevered anxiety.

Security came back gradually. It was not a feeling of complete security; rather was it a feeling that anything would be welcome if only it would happen. No policeman came prying round 53 Malcolm Road; no official from the hotel came to ask as to the present whereabouts of one James Medland. Marble had paid his debts, every one of them, like a sensible man, and that had taken all the slender store of one-pound notes. But his personal expenses were much higher nowadays—they were bound to be while he spent half a sovereign a day on whisky—and nothing he could say to Annie had any effect in reducing household expenditure. The old rule became well established of spending a little more than his income. Under such circumstances it was inevitable that the five-pound notes should begin to melt away. He was very careful about it, as his bank clerk experience taught him to be. Not one of those rustling pieces of paper ever passed through the hands of one of the local tradesmen, and most certainly never did one go through Mr Marble's account at the Bank.

Occasionally at the big, gilded, popular Corner Houses was to be seen a little round-faced man sitting alone. He ordered an expensive dinner, as expensive as the limited menu allowed, and he would eat it hurriedly and furtively, with never a glance from his pale-blue eyes at the people at the other tables, and having eaten he would call for his bill and hurry out. He paid the bill by means of a five-pound note, and, thrusting the change into his pocket, he would rush away as though pursued. So he was pursued, too. One pursuer was an impossible fear of one of the frock-coated floorwalkers stopping him and asking him whence came the note—with a meaning glance to an attendant to fetch the waiting detective—and the other was the haunting fear lest there might be someone casually finding out something in a desolate back garden in a dreary street in a southern suburb. Mr Marble learned what it meant to walk down that street with that foolish heart of his pounding away in his breast, hot with impatience to reach home to ensure that all would be well, and yet standing hesitating at his front gate unable to go in to face what might be there—police, or, what would be nearly as bad, a look in the eyes of his wife and children and words unspoken that meant that they *knew*. And still nothing happened.

The thing that came in the end was not in the least what he expected. It was nine o'clock in the evening, and Mr Marble was sitting in the same frowsty dining-room, from minute to minute gauging with his eye the two most important things of the moment—the height of the whisky in the bottle and the distance the hands of the clock had moved round. His wife was in the room too, but she made no sign of her presence save for her whispered conversation with herself. A smart rebuff from her husband earlier in the evening had shown her that it was not one of his 'nice' evenings. But when the postman knocked she rose and went to fetch what he had brought. It was only a single letter, and she gave it to Will. He fumbled it open with whisky-tangled fingers, and read the enclosed typewritten note with whisky-dazzled eyes. He read it three times before he understood the words, and for five minutes following he sat quite still as their significance came slowly home to him. It was formal notice to quit the house known as 53 Malcolm Road.

It was next morning before he could convince himself that the peril was not as real as his shrinking mind had believed last night. He was safe enough at present, of course. The Rent Act confirmed him in his tenancy for as long as it endured. This formal notice to quit was merely a necessary preliminary to raising his rent. But it gave him real cause for anxiety. It showed him a concrete thing to be afraid of, instead of the wild nightmares of prying neighbours or stray dogs, which might dig in that disused flower-bed. Some time or other he might be compelled to leave the house, and what would happen then? He did not know.

The next evening the librarian at the local Public Library had an interview with a little man in a seedy, blue suit, with a ragged, red moustache and weak blue eyes, who went through the formalities to obtain a ticket and then demanded a selection of books on crime.

'I am afraid we have very few books on the subject,' said the librarian, surprised.

'Never mind, let's see what you have got,' replied Marble.

The librarian brought him an armful of books. There were two of Lombroso's works, a volume of medical jurisprudence, two or three stray works on prison reform and kindred subjects, while from the bottom of the heap the librarian produced apologetically a rather lurid volume on *Crimes and Criminals: Historic Days at the Assizes*. Marble took the pile into his trembling hands, and peered at them anxiously.

'I'll have this one,' he said, firmly, *Crimes and Criminals* in his hand.

The librarian dated it and handed it over unwillingly. For one class of book borrower he had a friendly feeling; for another he had toleration, seeing that it was the main support of the library. The one class was that of the humble clerk and mechanic, anxious for self-improvement, the other was that of the diligent reader of fiction. For the omnivorous browser who read all sorts of things, he had a virulent hatred, suspecting him of a prurient desire to lay hold of those books which even a Public Library has to a small extent, the gift of some careless donor, or (dangerously, in his opinion) termed 'classical'. And this newcomer was evidently a bad example of this type. His perverted taste was obviously sated even with Public Library fiction, and the craving for sensation was worse, to his mind, even than the physiological researches of spotty-faced adolescents. He had taken the book of all the library of which the librarian was most ashamed. He shook his head sadly after the receding, bent-shouldered figure.

But that was the first night for months that Mr Marble did not drink more than was good for him. *Crimes and Criminals* held him fascinated. It was not a subject of which he knew very much; he was even ignorant of the details of ordinary criminal procedure. In this book he found criminals labelled as 'great'; he read ghastly stories of passion and revenge; he read of the final scenes on the scaffold with the dreadful concentration of a bird on a snake.

And the hair bristled on his head, and he experienced a horrible sensation of despair as he gradually realized that two out of every three of the criminals mentioned came to grief through inability to dispose of the body. There was a tale of a woman who had walked for miles through London streets with a body in a perambulator; there was an account of Crippen's life in London with the body of his murdered wife buried in his cellar; but the police laid hold of them all in time. On this damning difficulty the book dwelt with self-righteous gusto. At midnight Mr Marble put the book aside sick with fear. He was safe at present; indeed, he was safe altogether on many accounts. As long as he could see that that flower-bed was undisturbed no one would know that there was any cause for suspicion at all. That nephew of his had vanished into the nowhere that harbours so many of those whose disappearance is chronicled so casually in the papers. There was nothing, absolutely nothing, to connect him, the respectable Mr Marble, with young Medland's annihilation. But once let some fool start investigations, even involuntary ones, in that flower-bed, and the fat would be in the fire. Mr Marble did not know whether identification would be possible at this late date —he made a mental note that he must get another book from the library in which he could look that up—but even if that were impossible there would be unpleasant inquiries, and he would be in trouble for certain. Come what may, either he must maintain complete control over that flower-bed, or else he must make some other adequate arrangements. And from those 'arrangements', whatever they might be, his soul shrank in utter dread. They were certain to be his ruin. There would be some unforeseen mishap, just as there had been to the cart in which that man in the book tried to carry his victim's remains along Borough High Street. Then he would be found out and then——? Prison and the gallows, said Mr. Marble to himself, with the sweat pouring in torrents down his face.

One thing would give him security, and that would be the purchase of his house. That would give him security against disturbance for the rest of his life. Mr Marble did not mind what happened after his death, as long as that death was not accelerated by process of law.

But how could Mr Marble possibly purchase his house? He was living beyond his income as it was, he told himself, with a grim recollection of five-pound notes changed in Popular Corner Houses. Yet he must, he must, he must. The blind panic of the earlier months had changed to a reasoned panic now; the one object of Mr Marble's life now was to raise enough money to buy that house. The covering letter to yesterday's notice to quit had hinted that perhaps Mr Marble would find it to his advantage to buy instead of continuing to rent; Mr Marble went to bed, to toss and mutter at his wife's side all night long as he framed impossible schemes for acquiring money, a great deal of money, enough to buy the freehold of 53 Malcolm Road.

CHAPTER IV

At the Bank, as was only to be expected, they had noticed a slight change in Mr Marble's manner of late. He always looked worried, and clearly often he had been drinking. The head of the department to whom Mr Marble acted as second-in-command noticed it frequently, but he took no drastic action. For one thing, he was glad to have an inefficient second, as that enabled him to keep the work more closely under his own hand, thereby making his retention of his job more probable, and for another he had a queer sort of liking for 'poor old Marble', with his worried expression, and his worried eyes, and his worried moustache. In fact, Mr Henderson was heartily glad that Marble had apparently struggled out of the financial difficulties which had for many months before made him come to Henderson borrowing a fortnight before pay-day. What Henderson did not realize was that for all Marble's looseness of fibre, and seeming incompetence to grapple with anything worth while, somewhere in Marble there was a keen mind—razor keen still, despite too much whisky of late—and a fount of potential fierce energy which might contrive wonderful things if only something were to rouse him sufficiently. Mr Henderson, of course, knew nothing of a piece of work that Marble had performed marvellously efficiently some months ago.

So far Mr Marble had found no opportunity of making the money that he hankered after so pathetically. Yet money was in the air all the time that he was working, more so even than is usually the case in a bank department. For the department of the County National Bank, of which Mr Henderson was executive chief, with Mr Marble as his chief assistant, dealt solely with foreign exchange, buying and selling money all day, dollars for cotton spinners, francs for *costumiers*, pesetas for wine merchants, and dollars, francs, pesetas, and, above all, marks, for speculators of every trade or none. Gambling in foreign exchange was becoming a national habit by which the National County Bank profited largely. Here, if anywhere, would Mr Marble win the money for which he thirsted. But Mr Marble knew too much about foreign exchange operations, and he was afraid. There had been times when he had made a pound or two by well-timed buying and selling, but not many. He had the example before him of those who had bought marks at prices seemingly lower than they could ever be again, only to see them change from the absurd thousands to the still more absurd hundred thousands which meant the loss of nine-tenths of their investment. The wise man who speculated in foreign exchange would do well to sell, not buy, in most cases. And one could not sell without first buying unless one could arrange a 'forward operation' with a bank. One can only profit by a falling market if one sells what one has not got. And no bank would allow anyone to arrange a forward operation unless he could show some sort of reason for wanting to do so. Not much reason, of course, but a good deal more than a mere bank clerk with sixty pounds only in his account could possibly show. There was another advantage about the forward operation, too. It was only necessary in this case to put up a margin of ten per cent of one's investment. In that case an increase of five per cent in the value of the sum controlled meant an actual profit on the sum invested of fifty per cent—if one were lucky enough to have bought; if one had sold instead it meant a loss of fifty per cent. If a man were to buy on a ten per cent margin, and the money bought were to double in value, he would multiply the money invested not by two, but by twenty. Mr Marble thought of the sixty pounds he had to invest, and his mouth watered.

But week followed dreary week and nothing could be done. The foreign exchange market seemed to have gone mad. The mark had fallen away to millions, as the Austrian crown had done two years before. The lira seemed to be going the same way. Sterling exchange on New York alone was struggling back to its pre-war position. Even the franc was dropping steadily. Before the war it was little more than 25; now it was over a hundred, and it was being hammered slowly lower and lower. Mr Marble watched the market and hesitated. If the franc and the lira were to drop with a crash as the mark had done, and a wise man had sold in advance, he could look for a profit to be reckoned in terms of thousands per cent. And the brokers with whom Mr Marble in the course of his daily duties conversed over the telephone all seemed to think it likely. In the foreign exchange department of the National County Bank (Head Office) all the clerks were convinced of the same thing. Some of them had already made minute sums of money by cautious speculation, helped by their friends the clerks in the brokers' offices. They had sold tiny sums in advance, got out hurriedly immediately afterwards, and then cursed their faint-heartedness as the franc still went on dropping. Mr Marble saw all this, and was tempted. Twice he nearly ventured but each time that keen judgement of his which was always somewhere in the background ready to be called upon held him back. There was something doubtful somewhere.

And then one morning it happened. Chance flung a fortune within Mr Marble's reach, and only asked from him in return the effort to grasp it.

It was ten o'clock in the morning. Mr Marble was at his desk farthest from the entrance to the room, and close beside the partitioned cubbyhole that housed the superior majesty of Henderson, chief of the department. In front of Mr Marble lay the opened letters sent across by the correspondence department, and he was casually glancing through them to see that there was nothing that the department could not cope with without troubling Mr. Henderson, or even higher authority still. They were all just ordinary routine letters; notifications mainly, from the various continental branches, of credits given and of drafts honoured. Nothing of any import; the staff of the department could handle them nearly all. Four of them he picked out that he would have to answer; two must go in to Henderson. The last letter was the most ordinary of them all. It was the bi-weekly letter from the Paris branch confirming the actions reported already by cable and telephone. Mr Marble looked through it. Still there was nothing of any interest. For a wonder the Paris staff had made no mistake in decoding cables. Everything had been done as ordered, and no hasty cable would have to be sent countermanding some ridiculous blunder. No forgeries, no failures. Yet Mr Marble read the letter to the end, because the man who had written it was known to him personally; it was Collins, who had worked under him in that very department for a couple of years before being sent out to Paris. He was a voluble fellow—'chatty', Mr Marble described him to himself—and his volubility was noticeable even in this official correspondence, for at the end of the letter he had inserted a paragraph that was quite unnecessary by all rules of routine. It was quite brief for Collins, and merely said that more steadiness might be noticed in the French franc in future, as it was rumoured that the Government were taking the matter in hand, and might even resort to 'pegging' on the London exchange.

Mr Marble laid the letter down and gazed through the dusty window at the uninviting view of other dusty windows across the ventilation shaft. There might be something in it. The franc was a point higher this morning than at the close of yesterday. So much the trained foreign clerk's brain told him—Mr Marble could at two minutes' notice give the rate of exchange on anywhere at any time within the last two years—but Mr Marble was capable, strange though it may seem, of doing more than that if sufficiently stimulated. If the Republic took a hand in restoring its foreign credit, it would do more than merely keep it steady. Mr Marble suddenly recollected a nebulous idea he had framed some time ago as to the best means that would bring this about. He turned this idea over in his mind. If they were to do *that*, the franc would recover like a skyrocket. It would easily go to sixty; it might even reach fifty, or perhaps even forty. It would never be better than forty, decided Mr Marble, weighing the chances with an acuteness of perception that would have astonished him had he only thought about it. Most likely it would be about sixty.

'What's Paris now, Netley?' he asked a passing subordinate.

'One-nineteen, one-seventeen,' replied Netley over his shoulder as he hurried on hoping that Mr Marble would notice that he deliberately did not say 'sir'.

Two points rise again, thought Mr Marble. There might be some truth in the wild theories that had been flashing through his brain. On the other hand, it might be only one of the periodic and temporary recoveries that were usual. The price might sag at any minute again. If

Mr Marble were to buy, he might find that he had bought at the beginning of a fall instead of the beginning of a rise. And if he were to buy on a margin—Mr Marble had already in his mind a scheme to enable him to do so—then the inevitable ten point fall would deprive him of ninety per cent of his capital. But then—Mr Marble's silly heart was already bumping heavily against his ribs—the sort of rise he thought possible would bring him in nearly a hundred times the amount invested. Mr Marble managed to keep his brain deadly clear despite the thumping of his heart, just as he had done that memorable evening some months ago. It was a chance. Mr Marble's brain sorted out all the tiny indications it had collected and stored up unbidden for weeks past. It was more than a chance. It was a certainty, decided that clear brain.

Yet Mr Marble felt the flush of blood in his cheeks, and his heart beat unbearably as he rose from his seat and walked out of the office on what was to be one of the momentous occasions of his life. Even his gait was a little unsteady so great was the strain upon him, and the younger clerks whom he had to pass on the way to the door nudged each other merrily as he went by.

'Old Marble going out for his usual,' they said. 'Bit early even for him. Must have been properly soused last night.'

There was a public-house round the corner, and it was there that Mr Marble stayed his steps, just as, be it admitted, he had often done before. The girl at the bar knew him, and the double Scotch was ready for him before even he was within reach of it. But Mr Marble did not, as was usual, drain it off and demand another. Instead, he withdrew, glass in hand, to a bench behind a table, and sat waiting, waiting inexorably, while his heart beat in his finger tips so that his hands shook. It was only just opening time, and there was a steady stream of entrants, stockbrokers and clerks, street-betting agents, all the curious mixture that is to be found in a public-house fifty yards from Threadneedle Street on a weekday morning.

Once or twice men he knew entered, and nodded, but Mr Marble was not cordial. His return nod carried with it no invitation to share his bench and sit at his table with him. Most probably none of them would have accepted such an invitation anyway, unless it were unavoidable. Mr Marble continued to stare at the swing doors.

And then Mr Marble's heart gave a convulsive throb. He suddenly felt sick with fear, fear of the future. At last his scheme was presented to him in the concrete, instead of the comfortably abstract. For a wild moment he thought of flight, of abandoning the whole business. He could, he knew. He might struggle along for years without the aid that improbable success in this venture would bring him. But Mr Marble thrust the temptation on one side, and proceeded with the business with bitter determination. He beckoned to Saunders, the man whose entrance had caused this last internal commotion.

Saunders had his drink in his hand; he had greeted those men at the bar whom he knew, and was glancing round the room to make sure that he had missed no one.

He was a plump man of middle height, rosy and prosperous looking. He knew Marble slightly; that is to say, he had talked to him a dozen times in that public-house. He was acquainted with the fact that Marble worked for the National County Bank, which he himself employed, and that was all. Naturally he was a little puzzled at Marble's beckoning to him, but Saunders took care to be friendly to everyone who spoke to him, seeing that his livelihood depended on the goodwill of the public. Saunders was a bookmaker, in a tiny office five stories up near Old Broad Street, conducting his business almost entirely by telephone and by the men who waited about at lunchtime near the corners of the streets.

Glass in hand, Saunders came across to the table just as Marble had done before him, and almost without knowing it he sat down opposite him. There was that in Marble's manner which seemed to make it inevitable that he should sit down.

'Well,' said Saunders cheerily, 'how's things?'

'Not too bad,' said Marble. 'Got ten minutes to spare?'

Saunders supposed he had, a little ruefully, though, for he had at first imagined that this was merely evidence of a desire to open a credit account with him, and, since Marble's manner did not indicate this, he came to the other conclusion, that he was about to hear a 'hard luck story'. As far as Saunders' experience went, men between themselves did nothing but bet or borrow.

'You do bank with the National County, don't you?' began Marble.

'You're right.'

'And you know I work there?'

'Right again. What's the matter? Firm going bust? My account overdrawn?' Saunders was a witty fellow; there never was the slightest chance of the National County suspending payment, and Saunders' account was never lower than four hundred pounds. But Marble hardly smiled. Instead, he turned his bleak eyes full upon Saunders' brown ones.

'No,' he said; then slowly, 'I want to do a deal, and I must have the help of a customer of the bank. You'll do, or, of course, if you don't want to come in, I'll have to get someone else.'

'I should think you were right again,' said Saunders, but he was not feeling quite so full of levity now. His puzzled mind was searching for Marble's motives. Either this seedy old boy was balmy or else he was on some illegal lay. In either case Saunders was not having any.

Saunders was a law-abiding man, save in the matter of inciting others to street-betting. And yet—and yet——

'Do you want to hear about it?' said Marble, grimly. He had himself as well in hand as when he had offered Medland that glass of whisky, but the effort was frightful. His confidence overbore Saunders' easy scepticism.

'Right-ho. I don't say I'll buy it, though,' added Saunders hastily.

'No. But I want your word that you'll keep quiet if you don't.'

Saunders agreed. And the word of a bookmaker is accepted all over England.

'I've got some information. It might mean a lot of money if it were used properly.'

'Racin' information?' There was a suspicion of a sneer in Saunders' voice: he obtained half his income from people with racing information.

'No. Foreign exchange.'

'Don't hardly know what that is.'

'No,' said Marble. 'Lots of people don''

'Oh, I know a bit,' said Saunders, anxious to justify himself. 'I know about how the mark has fallen to half nothing and—and—all that sort of thing, you know.'

Somehow the moral tables had turned during those few minutes. Undoubtedly Marble was now in the ascendant. Largely, of course, this change was due to the fact that the conversation was about a subject of which he knew much and the other nothing. But on the other hand it must be admitted that the vague thing known as 'Personality' was affecting the case, too. Marble was putting out all his strength to influence Saunders unobtrusively, and he was succeeding. Men can do much when they have to.

'Well,' said Marble, bleak eyes set like stones, 'the franc is going to rise, and now is the time to buy.'

The secret was out now. Saunders could betray him

now at leisure. But Marble, never taking his eyes off Saunders', was sure he would not.

'I don't say you're not right,' said Saunders, 'but what's the little game? Where do I come in? And where do you come in?'

'It's like this,' said Marble, showing his whole hand, so sure was he. 'It isn't much good buying francs outright. I could do that myself next door. But you don't stand to make much that way. This time you might make a hundred per cent, but of course that's not good enough.'

'Of course not,' said Saunders submissively.

'The best way to do it is to make a "forward operation" of it. That means you must put up ten per cent.'

'On a margin,' put in Saunders, proud of this little bit of argot picked up during much frequenting of City public-houses.

'Exactly. On a margin. That means that a five per cent rise in the franc gives you fifty per cent profit. As I said, it might be a hundred per cent rise this time. That would be a thousand per cent profit—ten to one, in other words,' added Marble, countering Saunders' effort.

Saunders only dimly understood.

'But I don't see now why you're telling me all this,' he said. 'Why don't you get along and do it? Why tell anyone else at all?'

'Because I'm not allowed to put a forward operation through for myself in the Bank. You have to have some legitimate reason for wanting to.'

'And what reason would *I* have?' Saunders was being rapidly drawn into the net.

'Oh, that's easy. You can easily have some business in France, can't you? Don't you ever bet on French races?'

'Of course I do, sometimes.'

'And don't you ever send money to France?'

'Well, I have done, once or twice.'

'Right, then. If you were to tell the Bank that you

wanted to buy francs they'd believe you all right. And they love you in the Bank, anyhow. You keep a big current account, and they love anyone who does that.'

Saunders was still struggling against the mesmeric influence that was beginning to overpower him.

'Tell me some more about this "forward operation" stunt,' he pleaded, wavering, conscious that in a minute he would have to decide one way or the other, conscious that he would most probably fall in with Marble's plans, and conscious, too, that he did not really want to. 'Tell me what I should have to do.'

Marble explained carefully, drilling it into his man with meticulous care. Then he threw his last bait. He showed how, if a man were to take his profit when it amounted to a mere five times his stake, and had the hardihood to fling both profits and stake into the business again, by the time the currency purchased stood at twice the figure it stood at at the start the profit would not be ten, but thirty-five units.

Saunders scratched his head wildly.

'Here, what are you drinking?' he asked, signalling agitatedly to the barman, and then leaning forward again to go over the details once more. Marble's cold judgement had chosen his man well. A bookmaker earns his living by other people's gambling, but even with this practical example always before him there is no one on earth so ready to gamble—in anything not pertaining to the turf.

Then Saunders made a last despairing effort to writhe out of the business. He said that, after all, he was unacquainted with Marble.

'How do I know it's straight?' he asked pitifully.

'It can't be very well anything else, can it?' replied Marble, and the condescension in his tone was an added spur to Saunders. '*I* won't be able to pinch your money,

56

will I? It will all be in your account, won't it? If it isn't straight I can't make anything out of it.'

Saunders had realized this as soon as the words had left his mouth, and he apologized. Mr Marble, hope boiling in his veins, was very gracious.

'Well, what is it you want out of it?' asked the wretched Saunders.

'Ten per cent of what you make,' said Marble uncompromisingly, 'and, of course, I'm going to have a bit on, too.'

'How much?'

'Sixty quid.' Mr Marble produced a roll of five-pound notes—the last of those he had been so careful about changing. He was throwing discretion to the winds now. If ever the notes were traced to him, it would be his own fault, but there was no time for complicated manœuvres to change them.

Saunders took them half involuntarily.

'In fact,' said Mr Marble, 'I should like to have more than that on. Only I haven't got it with me. I could raise it by to-morrow. But to-morrow will be too late.'

With those baleful eyes upon him, and the reassuring feel of those five-pound notes in his hand, Saunders could do nothing except make the inevitable offer.

'Thanks,' said Marble. 'Look here, I tell you what we'll do. Put four hundred in. Two hundred of that will be yours. There's another sixty. Then you lend me the odd one-forty. That makes us just even.'

Saunders agreed helplessly.

'Time's getting on,' said Mr Marble, with a glance at the clock. 'We'd better get a move on. I can tell you what to do all over again as we walk back.'

As though in a dream Saunders rose from the table and followed him out. The stimulus of the fresh air outside revived him sufficiently to remember to ask

Marble how it was he was so certain that the franc was going to rise.

'I know all right,' said Marble casually. He could afford to be casual, so sure was he of himself, and above all, so sure was he of Saunders.

And Saunders weakly yielded to the man with the superior knowledge. He would have hooted with derision at a man who proposed to back a stray acquaintance's favourite horse to the tune of two hundred pounds; he would have rolled on the ground with mirth if he heard that the same man was going to risk another one hundred and forty by backing that horse for his friend; but this was not horse-racing, about which he was thoroughly well informed. It was business—Big Business—and he was awed and submissive.

Marble ended his instructions just as they reached the main door of the National County Bank.

'Go in there and say you want to buy francs as a forward operation. They'll send you along to my department, so don't worry. I'll be there. I may even do the business for you. But I expect it'll be Henderson that you see. Oh, yes, and don't forget, whatever you do, to ring me up two or three times to-day and to-morrow. Get through to Foreign Exchange and then ask for me. It doesn't matter what you say. Just say—what is that you always say when you see anyone in the bar?—"Hallo, old bean, how's things?" Keep it up for a bit; say "Doodle-oodle-oodle" if you can't think of anything else. That's just to give me authority to move the account about when it's necessary. Got it all? All right, then. Good-bye.'

Mr Saunders, dazed and mazed, walked weakly into the National County Bank. Mr Marble walked on to the side entrance where dwelt his own among other departments. The sweat was running off him in streams; for a brief space he had been a master of men; he had swayed a hard-headed man into doing something totally unexpected; he had gambled with fate and he had won; for a while he had known the wild exultation of success. He had done something that he would certainly not have done without the urgent impulse due to—a slight indiscretion one stormy night some months ago, but reaction closed upon him with terrible swiftness. His steps dragged as he came into the department of Foreign Exchange. He felt, and he looked, inexpressibly weary. The junior clerks nudged each other again as he walked by.

'Old Marble's had as much as he can carry already. He'll be getting the sack one of these days, just see if he doesn't.'

And Marble, tired to death, weary with fear, worn out by the thumping of his heart, crept brokenly to his desk and buried his face in his hands.

CHAPTER V

MR MARBLE was paying. He was paying by the feeling of weary misery from which he suffered as he walked that day across London Bridge, as he stood exhausted in the train, and in the bus which brought him from the station, and as he sat in the back room at 53 Malcolm Road.

It was a new habit this of sitting in the tiny 'drawing-room' instead of the dining-room. In the drawing-room the light was bad and the furnishing even more dreary than in the dining-room, while the fact that it was in the dining-room that during the winter they had their fire had habituated the family to passing all their time there. But Mr Marble now sat in the drawing-room. He did little enough there. He read, it is true, in the books that he now chose regularly from the Free Library— crime books, even the interminable *Lombroso*—but he only read at intervals. Quite half the time he spent in looking out of the window across the barren flower-bed. That way he felt more comfortable. He did not have to worry then in case some stray dog from one of the neighbouring houses were there. Mr Marble had read how dogs are employed to find truffles in Perigord and he was afraid.

There were in addition various children from neighbouring houses who had been known to climb into the garden after balls which they had knocked over. They had left off doing that now. Once upon a time Mr Marble had not shown any active objection, but two or three times lately he had caught them at it, and had rushed out in blind, wordless fury. The children had seen his face as he mouthed at them, and that experience was enough for them. Children know these things more clearly than do their elders, and they never came into Mr Marble's garden again. The neighbours were at a loss to understand Mr Marble's jealous guardianship of his garden. As they said, he never grew anything there. Gardening was hardly likely to be a hobby of a man with Mr Marble's temperament, and the garden of Number 53 had always been in its barren weediness an unpleasing contrast to those near it.

It gave at least some cause for a feeling of superiority to the neighbours. They all thought Mr Marble unbearably snobbish. He sent his children to secondary schools —on scholarships, it is true, and after some years at public elementary schools—while their children began to work for their livings at the age of fourteen, and he wore a bowler hat, while the neighbouring menfolk wore caps. They none of them liked Mr Marble, although they all had a soft corner in their hearts for Mrs Marble. 'Poor thing, he treats her like the dirt beneath his feet, he does.'

It was a comforting feeling that this monster suffered from the same troubles as they did, and was at times unable to pay his rent, even as they, for so the collecting clerk told them.

Mr Marble spent the evening sitting in the drawing-room of 53 Malcolm Road; on his knee was the last of the Free Library books on crime. It was very interesting —a *Handbook to Medical Jurisprudence*. Until he had begun it, Mr Marble did not know what Medical Jurisprudence was, but he found it more and more absorbing. The periods spent in gazing out of the window grew shorter and shorter as he read all about inquests, and the methods for discovering whether a dead body found in the water had been put there after death or not, and the legal forms necessary for certifying a person insane. Then he passed on to the section of Toxicology. He read all about the common domestic poisons, spirits of salt, lead acetate, carbolic acid; from these the book proceeded to the rarer poisons. The first ones mentioned, perhaps given pride of place because of infinitely superior deadliness, were hydrocyanic acid and the cyanides. The comments on the cyanides were particularly interesting:

'Death is practically instantaneous. The patient utters a loud cry and falls heavily. There may be some foam at the lips, and after death the body often retains the appearance of life, the cheeks being red and the expression unaltered.

'Treatment——'

But Mr Marble did not want to know anything about the treatment. Anyway, it was easy to see that there would rarely be an opportunity of treating a sufferer from cyanide poisoning. Besides, he did not want to read the book at all after that. It made his stupid heart beat too fast again, so that he had difficulty in breathing while his hand shook like the balance-wheel of a watch. And the book had started an unpleasant train of thought, that set him once again gazing out into the garden, only twilight now, at the end of the day, while he thought about blank horrors.

He knew much more about crime than when he had first become a criminal. He knew that nine murderers out of ten were only discovered through some silly mistake. Even if they were very careful about planning the deed, and carried it out successfully, they still made some ridiculous blunder that betrayed them. But in some cases they were found out by some unfortunate mischance. It was generally through the gossip of neighbours, but sometimes it was through the insatiable curiosity of some really uninterested person. Now Mr Marble could rely upon there being no gossip. No one knew that young Medland had come to his house that night. And he had made no blunder. It was only some event beyond his control that could betray him. Such as? The answer came pat to mental lips—someone else moving into the house after he had been turned out, *someone with a taste for gardening*. Come what may, he must not be turned out of 53 Malcolm Road. But he might be at any minute now. His tortured mind raced like a steamship propeller in a rough sea. Supposing the franc should fall! He would lose his money, but that would be only part of his loss, and the least part, too. For Saunders would complain about his loss, perhaps even to the management of the Bank, certainly in a way that would come to the ears of the authorities. Then Marble would lose his job—not possibly, but certainly. Then—a few weeks of grace perhaps, and then, rent unpaid, out of the house he would go. After that it was inevitable. Mr Marble shuddered uncontrollably. It all depended on the franc. One part of Mr Marble's feverishly active mind began to toil once more through all the data accumulated that had made him decide that the franc would rise; another part began to regret bitterly that he had ever entered into such an absurd venture, rashly leaving his temporary safety— which already he began to long for again—in a wild search for permanency. Perhaps this was his blunder, like Crippen's flight to the Continent. Perhaps it was because of this that he was going to be hanged by the neck till he was dead. That other book, the one about Famous Criminals, had been disgustingly fond of that expression. Mr Marble shuddered again.

Mr Marble sat till late that night—indeed, he sat until early the next morning, disregarding, hardly hearing the appeals of his wife, working out with one part of his mind the chances of the rise of the franc, with the other the chances of escaping detection. Mr Marble found some ghoulish details at the end of the *Handbook to Medical Jurisprudence* which interested him as well as appalled him. They dealt with the possibilities of identifying bodies after prolonged burial.

At half-past seven the next morning, Mr Marble, who was already awake—he hardly seemed to sleep nowadays —heard the newspaper pushed through the letterbox of the front door downstairs. He climbed out of bed and padded down barefooted and in his pyjamas. The house was very still, and it seemed as if the beating of his heart shook it. It was unfortunate that it should start again now when it had taken him all the time he was in bed to quiet it down. But there was no help for it. Mr Marble wondered whether the paper had anything to say about the franc, and of course that was enough to start it.

With the fibre doormat scratching his bare feet Mr Marble stood and read the financial columns of the newspaper. It was unenlightening. It mentioned the closing price of the franc—118—one point better than he had bought at. Mr Marble knew that already. Nowhere was there any mention of drastic action by the French Government. Everything seemed as it was yesterday. Mr Marble realized that he might perhaps be able to get out of the transaction even now with safety and a small profit. That would perhaps keep Saunders' mouth shut. But Mr Marble only dallied with the idea for a moment. Then his eyes narrowed, and his weak, nubbly chin came forward an eighth of an inch. No. He would stick it out now. He would carry the business through, cost what it might. He was sick of being afraid. There was some quite good stuff in the make-up of Mr William Marble. It was a pity that it took danger of life and death to stir him up to action.

Yet Mr Marble was so anxious that he called up to his wife, 'Aren't you *ever* coming down, Annie?' and he bustled hastily through his dressing and breakfast and rushed off to the City a good half-hour before his usual time. No one in the crowded railway carriage guessed that the little man in the blue suit perched in the corner, his feet hardly touching the floor, who read his paper with such avidity, was hastening to either fortune or ruin, although perhaps a closer glance than ever Mr Marble received might have raised some strange speculations, considering his white face and his tortured light-blue eyes. He did not walk across the bridge from the station. Instead he scampered, breathlessly.

At the Bank he hung up his hat and coat carelessly, and dashed upstairs to the department of Foreign Exchange. The few clerks already there stared in wonder at his unwontedly early arrival. Straight to Mr Henderson's room went Mr Marble, to that private sanctum which only he and Henderson had the right to enter. He looked at the tape machine. Fool that he was! Of course, there would be no quotations through yet. He might as well have stayed at home.

He came back to his desk, and sat down, making a pretence of being busy, though this was difficult to maintain, as the letters had not yet arrived. He waited for twenty minutes while the room filled with late arrivals of the one time-table and the early arrivals of the other. The customary din of the office began to develop. The telephones began to ring, and the clerks began to call to each other from desk to desk. Mr Marble became conscious that young Netley was speaking into the telephone opposite. He knew from Netley's greeting to the unknown at the other end that he was talking to the exchange brokers in London Wall.

'Yes,' said Netley, 'yes, no, what, really? No, I hadn't heard, yes, yes, all right.'

Marble knew instinctively what he was talking about.

'What's Paris now, Netley?' he asked.

Netley was so full of his surprising news that he did not notice the coincidence, and also actually added the hated 'sir'.

'Ninety-nine, sir,' he said. 'It's gone up twenty points in the night. They don't know why, yet.'

Marble knew. He was right, of course. He had a good head for finance when he chose to use it.

Henderson came in and passed through to his own room. Marble did not notice him. He was busy thinking. He was nerving himself to go on with the venture. If he sold now he could give Saunders some three hundred pounds profit—enough to satisfy him most probably. Anyway, he was safe for a bit. Keeping in close touch with the market as he naturally did, he could sell at the instant a decline seemed likely. But if he did what he had suggested to Saunders yesterday—sold out and then re-invested, he would be much less safe. A ten per cent drop would wipe out profit and capital as well, and

Saunders would think he had been swindled. But all Marble's judgement told him that the rise was bound to continue. There was a huge gain to be made if only he was bold enough—or desperate enough—to risk it. Henderson appeared at the door of his room.

'Mr Marble,' he said, 'someone wants you.'

Marble went in and picked up the receiver.

'Hullo,' he said.

'That Mr Marble?' said the receiver.

'Hallo, old bean, how's things?' said the receiver.

It was Saunders. He had begun to regret his transaction of the previous day long ago, but he was determined on playing the game to the last. Marble might have got four hundred pounds out of him by some nefarious means, but he was not going to get a rise out of him as well. He would see the thing through to the bitter end.

'Going well,' said Mr Marble.

He had to pick his words, for Henderson was within earshot, and it would never do for him to know that he was acting in collusion with one of the Bank's customers.

'They've begun to rise,' said Mr Marble. 'Look at your tape machine.'

Mr Saunders was unable to retain an exclamation of surprised unbelief.

'You can get out now with a bit of profit,' said Mr Marble. His tone was cold and sincere, as he was striving to make it, and carried conviction.

'Sorry, I can't hear what you're saying,' said Mr Marble.

'Doodle—oodle—oodle,' said the receiver, as Mr Saunders realized that this was his cue, and all his old gambling spirit came back to him.

'Right. I think you're wise,' said Mr Marble, replacing the receiver.

'That Mr Saunders,' said Marble to Henderson. 'Bought some francs yesterday—lucky devil—wants to sell and reinvest.'

In the outer office the usual nerve-racking bustle was at its usual height. Mr Marble sat at his desk, where the letters had now been put, and rallied himself. For nearly five minutes he fought with himself before he could turn to the telephone at his elbow and give the necessary orders to increase Saunders' holding—and the risk as well.

There was apparently no need to worry. Mr Marble sold at 95; he bought again at 93. Half an hour later the franc stood at 87, and the risk was past. It is an old story now, how the French Government had quietly appropriated other people's credits the night before, how the franc rose all day long, while puzzled exchange-brokers racked their brains to explain the mystery, and cursed their gods that they had not foreseen this action and bought all the francs that their credit would stand. And all day the franc rose, as men who had been caught hurried in to cover their losses, as the German speculators who had been hammering away so joyfully gave up the struggle in despair, as the small investors who follow the movements of the market far to the rear came panting in to steal a slice of profit as well. The men in the office who only a few days before had been confidently predicting that the franc would go the way of the mark had already changed their minds completely and were now saying that it would climb to its pre-war value of twenty-five and a quarter. But Mr Marble kept his head, just as he had kept it that fatal night when he knew that a single mistake meant ruin and violent death. The cold fear that had succeeded to the initial feeling of elated success vanished completely, and he was left calm, deadly calm. He watched the market with a fierce intensity. Once or twice it wavered, as the faint hearts took their profits, but each time it recovered, as it was bound to do with a genuine demand behind it. At 75 he resold and reinvested again, sitting lunchless in the office all

day, so as to keep the business under his own hand, and when the franc touched 65 he sold out for good. It might well go a little higher, as indeed it did, reaching 60 for a brief space, but he had done all that was necessary and a good deal more.

There was no need to work out the profit. He knew that already, counting with painful eagerness every penny that every point meant to him. He called to the department stenographer, and began the official Bank letter to Saunders reporting the progress made:

Dear Sir,
In accordance with your instructions received to-day by telephone at 9.45 a.m. and 4.51 p.m. we have——

and all the rest of the business. It was cold and dry and formal enough, heaven knew. Bank letters are usually cold and dry and formal, even when they embody a pæan of praise. This one told, with an air of supreme detachment, how Mr Saunders had originally bought rather more than forty-five thousand francs with the four thousand pounds represented by his margin of four hundred; how they had been sold at 95, and then represented nearly five thousand pounds (a thousand pounds profit); how this thousand pounds, and the original four hundred, had purchased francs at 93, and thus, thanks to the fact that each pound did the work of ten, controlled nearly a million and a quarter of francs; this million odd had been sold at 75, bringing in sixteen thousand pounds and more. Mr Saunders' profit now stood at over four thousand pounds, and it and the good old original four hundred had gone back once more into francs, purchased at 75 still, thanks to Mr Marble having taken advantage of an eddy in the market. Forty-five thousand pounds' worth of francs did that sum control—three millions of francs and a few thousand odd ones.

When they were finally sold at 65 Mr Saunders' credit

balance stood at a paltry fifty-one thousand pounds. He probably was unable to do the simplest sum in foreign exchange; at the moment he did not have the least idea of what profit he had made; Marble's forethought had earned it for him; most of the money would come eventually out of the pockets of less fortunate speculators, which only served them right, but some would come from the myriad firms which had to have francs at any price. Above all, if the Bank had had anything to say in the matter they would probably have cut short the speculation at the earliest opportunity, but they had never been consulted after the first interview. Mr Marble had a specious plea of justification for having done all this on his own responsibility, in that Henderson had acquiesced in the first expansion of the deal, but he did not think he would have to use it. No bank really objects to having its clients enriched by the enthusiasm of its staff.

When the letter was finished Mr Marble slipped out of the office. He had done no work that day, and he would not have been able to even if he had tried. He was too exhausted by the emotional strain under which he had been labouring all these hours. Instead, he walked quietly round to Saunders' office. The hurrying crowds round him, hastening to catch the 5.10 at Fenchurch Street, or the 5.25 at London Bridge, did not pay him the tribute of a glance. They did not realize that this shabby man in blue was a capitalist—a man possessed of over ten thousand pounds, *if he could be sure of making Saunders pay up*. They paid no heed to him, save to shoulder their homeward progress. He was rich almost to the full extent of his wildest dreams, and yet they pushed him into the gutter. Mr Marble did not resent it. They had likewise paid no heed to him when he was only a murderer.

Saunders in his office, the last race of the day over,

was glancing through some trial totals of the day's figures when one of his two clerks showed in Mr Marble.

'Hallo?' he said, glancing up, 'so you've made a bit?'

Mr Marble sank wearily into the chair indicated and took the cigarette that Saunders offered.

'What did you get? Six to one?' asked Saunders. He was half joking, half serious. He had determined that Mr Marble's final bait of yesterday of three thousand per cent was a mere piece of bluff. Obviously Marble had taken a chance and it had come off, and he, glad to see his money back, let alone with profit attached, would not press him too hard for the fulfilment of all his promises.

'Don't know,' said Marble. 'Haven't worked it out like that. But the total comes to something like fifty thousand.'

'What?' gasped Saunders. 'Fifty thousand? Or it's francs, I suppose you mean?'

'No,' said Marble expressionlessly, 'pounds.'

'D'you mean it?'

'Oh, of course I do. You'll get the official notification from the Bank to-morrow.'

Saunders said nothing. Nothing in his limited vocabulary was equal to the situation.

'Fifty thousand pounds,' said Mr Marble, still expressionless, but bracing himself unobtrusively for the final effort. 'Let's work out what my share of it is.'

It was astonishing to him to find that Saunders agreed without any difficulty at all. He would not have been surprised to find him refusing to render any account whatever; he could have retained the whole and nothing could have been proved against him. But Marble, when he feared this, allowed his fear to overbalance his estimation of several important items in Saunders' make-up. In the first place, Saunders was an honest man. In the second place, he was so dazzled by the magnitude of the profit that he did not grudge the fair share of the man who had earned it for him. In the third place, he was a bookmaker, and he was accustomed to handing over large sums on account of transactions of which no law in the United Kingdom took the slightest notice.

'Rightio,' said Saunders. 'How much is it exactly?'

'Fifty thousand, three twenty-nine, and a few shillings.' Saunders hastily figured it out. Marble had done it in his head long ago.

'I make your little packet come to £27,681. Oh, and the sixty you gave me. I get twenty-two thousand odd for myself. Not bad going for three phone calls.'

Saunders was trying to be offhand in the presence of this magician who could make thousands sprout in the course of a night. Actually, he was bursting with astonishment and curiosity.

'When's settling day?' he demanded.

'The money'll come in soon. You'll have it in less than a week. Might be to-morrow, but I doubt it. The Bank will let you know.'

'Right. I'll send you a cheque then. Your working agree with mine?' Saunders was trying his best to be the complete business man, although the largest cheque he had written in his life was for no more than five hundred pounds, and that occasion still haunted him in his worst nightmares.

'Very well, then.' Mr Marble rose from his chair.

Mr Saunders could retain himself no longer.

'Oh, sit down, man, and tell me how it was done. No, we must go and have a drink to celebrate this. Let's make a night of it, up West somewhere. Let's——'

But none of these things appealed to Mr Marble, although the very mention of a drink set him yearning.

'No,' said Mr Marble. 'I have to push off home.'

And he went home, too. Although Mr Marble was possessed of twenty-seven thousand pounds he spent his evening, as long as he was sober, sitting in a dreary little suburban drawing-room gazing out over a desolate suburban backyard, for fear lest some trespasser or some stray dog should find something out.

CHAPTER VI

MR MARBLE arrived home one evening lighter of step and of heart than he had been for some time previously. Even when the shadow of the gallows lies across one's path one cannot help feeling a little elated when one has just received, and paid into a new account at a new bank, receiving the homage of a bank manager, the sum of twenty-seven thousand pounds odd.

Mr Marble was done with speculation. The money, as he had decided in a serious conference with the bank manager, was all going into gilt-edged investments—save for a thousand pounds which was destined for the purchase of 53 Malcolm Road. Even with this deduction Mr Marble would be in the possession of the comfortable income of twelve hundred pounds a year, although—as the bank manager said deprecatingly—the income-tax collector would have a fat slice out of it.

So Mr Marble hung up his hat in the hall with a freedom of gesture unusual to him, and marched briskly into the dining-room to find his family assembled still over the tail end of their tea.

'You're early, Will,' said Mrs Marble, rising uncomplaining to hurry the preparation of her husband's evening meal.

'So I am, so I am,' said Mr Marble, and threw himself down in the armchair beside the empty grate.

It is a strange fact, but true, that Annie Marble's habit of saying the obvious did not get on his nerves. In that lukewarm wooing, seventeen years ago, one of the things that appealed most strongly to Mr Marble was the fact that Annie did not say unexpected things, and that he never had to bother about entertaining her. Yet at the moment he had a little scene in his mind's eye that would startle her and interest her enormously, and he had been looking forward to it for days.

'What about school, John?' he said.

John leisurely drank tea before replying. It was his way.

'All right,' said John. He did not use three words where two would do.

Mr Marble had guessed already that John would have little to say, and the idea pleased him, for he knew that his next words would force him into saying something more than usual.

'You'll be leaving at the end of this term, John,' he said.

John put down his cup with a slight clatter and stared at his father.

'Really?' he said.

Only one word this time. Somehow it irritated Mr Marble.

'Yes. I shall be entering you for the College next term.'

Mr Marble was doomed to disappointment. John said nothing for a while. He was too stunned to speak. Nearly four years at his secondary school had endeared the place to him, and he had begun to look forward to the alluring prospect of prefectship and 'colours'. This cup had been rudely snatched from his lips. And he was to be sent to the College. Sydenham College was a public school, one of the second rank only, though this subtle distinction did not matter to John at that age, and there was no love lost between the secondary foundation and this lordly place, whose boys rode on motor-bicycles, and turned up their noses at the rest of humanity.

It was this that made the sharpest appeal to John's dumb but sensitive little soul. At Sydenham College he would be torn apart from the friends he had made during four long summers. He, too, would have to turn up his nose at Manton and Price and good old Jones, whose glasses were always bent the wrong way. He wouldn't, of course, but—he realized this with a flash of prophetic insight—they would *expect* him to and that would be just as bad. For the moment John saw things very clearly. At the College he would be received and treated like a secondary boy, and at the School there would be instinctive hostility towards him. He would not be fish, nor fowl, nor good red herring.

'Oh, say something, for goodness' sake,' said Mr Marble, pettishly. 'Don't sit there staring like a stuffed dummy.'

John addressed his eyes to his plate. 'Thank you, father,' he said.

'Confound it, boy,' said Mr Marble, 'anyone would think you didn't *want* to go there. The finest public school in England, and you're going there. And'—here Mr Marble threw his finest bait—'if you get on well there and distinguish yourself, there might be that motor-bike I've heard you talking about, some day.'

But the effort was vain. Even a motor-bicycle meant nothing to John if it was conditional upon his going to the College. If Mr Marble had only mentioned it before he had mentioned the other, John's reception of the suggestions might have been different. As it was, John could only mumble 'thank you' again and fidget with the crumbs on his plate. Mr Marble turned from him exasperated, and addressed his real favourite, Winnie, instead.

'And you, miss,' he said, with a jocosity which, unwonted as it was, had precisely the opposite effect to the one he desired, 'what do you want most?'

It was an unsatisfactory question to put suddenly to an unprepared fourteen-year-old even if she was nearly fifteen. Winnie thought and fumbled with her dress, and looked away as she became conscious of the concentrated gaze of everyone in the room. To her aid came the recollection of what she most envied the biggest girl in her form.

'Green garters,' she said.

Mr Marble roared with laughter, only the tiniest bit forced.

'You'll have a lot more than that,' he laughed. 'We'll be buying you a new outfit altogether this week, lock, stock, and barrel. What do you say to going away to a nice school, a real young ladies' school, where as likely as not you'll ride a horse in the mornings, and have all the things you fancy, and be friends with lords' daughters?'

'Ooh, I should like that,' said Winnie, but it was only modified rapture. Mr Marble had sprung his little surprise too surprisingly to have the effect he desired. But he was satisfied for the moment.

'But is this all true?' asked Winnie. 'Are we really all going to have just what we like?'

'As true as true. We can have just whatever we like,' said Mr Marble, overjoyed to find Winnie, at least, impressed.

'Well, what's mummie going to have?' continued Winnie.

Mr Marble turned to his wife, who had sat behind his shoulder, suddenly, when she heard this surprising conversation begin. Mr Marble looked at his wife, and she began to think, confusedly, as always.

'Anything I want at all?' she asked, more to gain time than from any other motive.

'Anything you want at all,' repeated Mr Marble.

Mrs Marble let her mind travel free, without hindrance from the strait limits of expense which had hedged it in all her life. And her thoughts flew straight, as they often did, to green fields and the sunlight in the hedgerows. With the clearness of mental vision so often granted to those of stumbling intellect a picture rose before her mind's eye of a sunny, hyacinth-scented lawn, full of the murmuring of bees, sleepy little hills, half-wooded, in the distance, and Mr Marble beside her, kind and a little attentive and loverlike.

'Oh, do be quick, mummie,' said Winnie.

Mrs Marble translated her thoughts to the best of her ability.

'I want a new house and a nice garden,' said Mrs Marble.

Mr Marble made no comment. He was so silent that in time they all turned and looked at him. He had shrunk back in his chair, literally shrunk, so that he only seemed to be half the bulk he had been when he came in. His face was blank, and his lips moved without uttering a sound. He rallied in the end.

'You won't have that,' he said. 'You'll never have that.'

Then he guessed at the strangeness of his manner from their surprised expressions, and tried to mask it.

'Houses are hard to get these days,' he said. 'And I'm sure I'm fond enough of the old house not to want to leave it. Can't you think of something else, Mother?'

Of course Mother could, if Will wanted her to. Discussion began in a more animated form, as they warmed to the subject.

Even John was in the end lured into joining in. Suggestions were bandied back and forth—furniture for the house, motor-cars, theatres, chicken for dinner on Sundays. But somehow they all avoided the crying need the house was in for redecoration, and none of them suggested obtaining the assistance of a jobbing gardener to put some beauty into the backyard. Three of those present didn't know why. It was instinctive.

As Mr Marble recovered his good spirits, he became more jovial and friendly than the children could remember his being for years. They chuckled when he produced a big notebook and made a show of noting down all the suggestions offered.

'But your tea's getting cold, Will,' said Mrs Marble. 'Why don't you have it now and go on with the game after?'

The children looked anxiously at their father. Was it after all just a game? It would be too bad if it were. But he reassured them at once.

'It isn't a game, mother,' he said, 'it isn't, really.'

But still Mrs Marble looked her unbelief. Half buried in her tangled memory there were one or two recollections of times when her husband had cruelly taken advantage of her dimness of thought. And she was sensitive about it, and shrank from having it exposed once more.

'It isn't a game, mother,' said John and Winnie, encouraged.

'I've just made a pot of money in the City,' said Mr Marble.

'Father's just made a pot of money in the City,' repeated Winnie.

Gradually she came to believe them.

'How much?' she asked, astonishingly more practical than her children.

'More than you could guess,' said Mr Marble, adhering

firmly to his article of faith that under no conditions should one's wife know anything about one's income—although this had once before brought him to the verge of ruin. 'Enough to keep us all our lives,' added Mr Marble, rubbing it in.

'But you're not—you're not going to give up the Bank?' said Mrs Marble, aghast. You could feel that capital letter as she spoke. Awe for the vast institution which gave them their daily bread, and terror of the Damocles' sword of dismissal which dangled always over their heads were ingrained into her being from the early days of marriage.

'I don't know yet,' said Mr Marble easily. 'I may and I may not.'

'Oh, Will, you mustn't, you mustn't really. Supposing anything went wrong.'

'Wrong? What's going to go wrong?' Marble could not keep a suspicion of a sneer out of his voice. He was nettled at the suggestion that anything should 'go wrong' with financial affairs under his control, after his astonishing feat of manipulation of the franc. He did not make full allowance for the fact that Mrs Marble knew nothing of this. That was perhaps characteristic, and equally so was his annoyance that she should interfere in the slightest with his control of their joint lives.

'I don't know, but—oh, Will, you can't have made as much money as all that?'

'Can't I! I have.'

To children it seems perfectly natural that their father should come home one day and say that he has made all their fortunes; but to a woman nothing seems more unlikely than that the husband should say the same thing. It took a long time to convince Mrs Marble. Indeed, by the time that this was done, Mr Marble had lost all enjoyment. Nobody had been very enthusiastic; nobody had told Mr Marble what a very wonderful man he was; John, indeed, had seemed positively sorry that it had happened. And Mrs Marble had said the deplorably wrong thing—as of course was only to be expected. Poor Marble's long-stretched nerves gave way, and he ended by losing his temper rather badly.

'You're a lot of fools,' he snapped. 'As for you, Annie ——'

Annie wept, and as always when that happened Mr Marble could bear things no longer. He uttered an inarticulate noise which only inadequately conveyed his disgust, and rose indignantly from his chair. Then he went through a series of actions which Annie and the children had come to know all too well. He roamed round the room and picked up a couple of the eternal books on crime that lay about; then he felt in his pocket for the sideboard key; he brought from the sideboard the decanter, the siphon, and the glass; and then with his arms full he passed out of the room. The children and their mother heard him go into the drawing-room at the back, and they heard the door shut with unnecessary violence.

'Oh dear, oh dear, oh dear,' wailed Mrs Marble, handkerchief to her eyes. Then she rallied. It was still an article of faith with the Marble family that the head of the house did not drink, never had drunk, and a thousand times never had been the worse for drink. And at the same time another article of faith had grown up lately. That was that Mr Marble did not sit all those hours in the drawing-room for any particular purpose. It was just a little whim of his, unaccountable, but not to be commented upon.

'Now, children,' said Mrs. Marble, determined at all costs—although she did not know why—to enforce these beliefs, and at the same time to hold up the prestige of her husband, 'get on quietly with your homework and don't make a noise to disturb father. Perhaps he'll tell us more about it when he's not so tired.'

She rose from the table and gathered up the tray on which still lay her husband's untasted tea. She went out quietly, tip-toeing past the drawing-room door. A good part of the evening she spent in washing up. The rest she spent in ironing.

When at last she had done her work, and had seen the children off to bed she came and sat down quietly in the deserted dining-room. She was very tired, and she was very worried. Of course, she believed dear Will when he said he had made all that money, but still—he might have made a mistake somewhere, and it might not be as he thought. She felt very frightened about his obvious determination to leave the Bank. Not for all the wealth Will said he had made would she admit to herself that the main cause of her worry was the haunting suspicion that perhaps Will had made this money illegally. He might be taken away and put in prison. That would be terrible, but, of course, she would always love him and be true to him. Indeed, Mrs Marble, thinking in muddled fashion but doggedly as was her wont, decided that something like this must have happened. He had not really done anything wicked of course, but there would be suspicions against him, and all the evidence would point that way, and so on. His recent anxiety, which even Mrs Marble had guessed at, and his mutterings at night as he lay at her side all seemed to prove the same thing. Poor boy, he must be very worried. And the thought of him sitting there all alone in the half-dark drawing-room moved her to vast pity. All her queer love for him rose in her breast and she felt her eyes growing moist. She loved him very, very dearly. It was because of this anxiety of his that he had not been as tender towards her as he had once been. But that would end now, now that he knew that she was on his side and shared his trouble.

There was nothing in the world so dear to Mrs Marble as the kisses of that little, shabby man with the reddish moustache, who bore the fires of hell eternally in his bosom. With her love welling up in her breast until it began even to oppress her, so that she had to rest her hand over her heart, Mrs Marble came to the cross-roads of her life—and did not even know that she had reached them. Without further thought she went out of the room, and quietly across into the other, bearing love and hope to her darling husband.

He was sitting in the position that had become habitual, in the uncomfortable late Victorian armchair, facing the window and about two yards from it. His position indicated an awkward compromise between tension and relaxation. On the chair beside him stood his whisky and his glass, and on his lap lay his book, as if he had interrupted his reading for a moment to follow some train of thought which had just occurred to him. But for the last hour nearly, it had been too dark to read. Mr Marble was half drunk, and his mind was working out possibilities of unimaginable horror, as he gazed out into the nearly dark garden which held his secret.

'Dear,' began Mrs Marble, and then, as he did not answer: 'Are you awake, dear?'

She came nearer to him, walking like a grey ghost in the semi-darkness, and touched him lightly on the shoulder. Mr Marble sprang into instant activity. He writhed in his chair, and the whisky decanter went over with a crash, sending its scant contents gurgling out on to the carpet.

'What—what——' he spluttered. After all, a man can be ready for all emergencies only for a limited time, and Mr Marble had relaxed for once. Then he saw that it was only his wife. 'Oh, it's you, you fool,' he snarled, ashamed of his absurd fear—he would not admit to himself what he had been afraid of—and angry with her, with himself, and with everything else.

'Oh Will, I'm so sorry,' said Mrs Marble, stooping to pick up the decanter, her slippers sopping with whisky.

A bare half-inch remained in the decanter—mere mockery. Mr Marble peered at it, and swore. It was an ugly word he used, and Mrs Marble drew her breath in sharply. But she still tried to make the peace.

'Never mind, Willie boy,' she said, 'I couldn't help it. Your can get some more in the morning. Never mind, dear.'

They were the little pathetic words she used to use when John was a little boy, very near to her heart, and something had upset him. To Mrs Marble's mind the loss of his whisky must affect Mr Marble in the same way as did a broken toy affect Baby John.

'Never mind, dear,' said Mrs Marble, and she put out her hand to his forehead, just as she used to do.

But Mr Marble only pushed her away pettishly, and growled out the ugly word he had used before. It was that that upset Mrs Marble. She was used to his fits of temper—she would not have loved him so dearly had he not had them, baby like—but he had never sworn at her, never before. Still she made another effort, trying to get past his outstretched arm to touch his forehead and ruffle back the sparse hair in the way she loved doing.

'That wasn't what I wanted to speak about, dear,' she said. 'I wanted——'

'I hope to God it wasn't,' sneered Marble. 'You would be a bigger fool than even I thought you were if you came in here just to upset my whisky.'

'Oh, Willie, Willie,' sobbed Mrs Marble. She was crying now.

'Oh, Willie, Willie,' mocked Mr Marble, his nerves fretted red raw.

'No, Willie, *do* listen. I wanted to tell you that I know about it, after all, and it doesn't matter. It doesn't matter a bit, dear. It won't alter me at all.'

She was able to say this long speech—long for her, that is—only through the inability of her husband to say or do anything. He had gripped the arms of the chair and was staring at her in terror. Then at last he spoke, or rather croaked. His throat was dry and his heart was pounding away in his breast like a steam engine.

'How—how do you know?'

'I don't know really, dear, I just guessed. But you don't understand, dear. It doesn't matter, that's what I wanted to say.'

Marble laughed; it sounded horrible in the darkness.

'So you think it doesn't matter? A lot you know.'

'No, dear, I don't mean that. I mean it doesn't matter my knowing. Oh, Willie dear——'

But Marble was laughing again. It was a wild beast sound.

'If *you* could guess, half the world will guess to-morrow. Ah——'

'To-morrow? Don't they know now?'

'Would I be here if they did, you fool?'

'No, dear. But I thought perhaps they suspected.'

'There's nothing for them to suspect. They can only know.'

'But how can they know?'

'If young Medland——'

'Medland? Oh, you mean that young nephew who came here. Did he help you? I've often wanted to ask you about him.'

Marble stared at her grey form in the twilight. He could not see her face, and he felt a horrid fear that either she was tempting him or else he had lost his unassailable position for a silly nothing. For a moment the first idea triumphed.

'You devil,' he said. 'What are you doing? What are you asking me this for?'

His voice cracked with fear and passion. Mrs Marble said nothing. She was too startled to utter a word. Mr Marble stared at her unmoving figure, and for a moment a wild, ridiculous fear of the unknown overwhelmed him. Was it really his wife, or was it—was it—? Blind panic began to overmaster him. He struck out wildly at the brooding form. He felt a savage pleasure as his fist struck firm flesh, and he heard his wife give a startled cry. He struck again and again, heaving himself up out of his chair to do so. The little chair fell over, and the glass and the siphon broke into a thousand clattering fragments. His wife screamed faintly as he followed her across the room, hitting with puny savagery.

'Oh, Willie, Willie, don't!'

Then chance directed a blow more accurately and Mrs Marble fell dumbly to the ground.

Marble staggered, and clutched the back of a chair to steady himself. As his panic passed, he was only conscious of a dreadful weakness; and he could hardly stand, and he was dizzy with strain and with the pounding of his heart. There came a clattering outside the room, and then the door was flung open. The light from the hall lamp outside streamed in, revealing John standing by the door in his ragged nightclothes. His mother lay where she had fallen, close at his feet.

For a second father and son stared at each other. It was only for a second, but that was enough. At the end of it John knew that he hated his father; and his father knew that he hated his son. John opened his mouth to speak, but no words came. Then his mother at his feet sighed and stirred. Mr Marble recovered himself with an effort—oh, those efforts!

'Glad you came down, John,' he said. 'Your mother's had a—bit of an accident. Help me upstairs with her.'

John said nothing, but he bent and put his arm under her shoulders, while Marble held her at her knees. Between them they dragged her upstairs. She was conscious and well enough to walk up herself by that time, but a frozen silence lay on all three of them, and none of them would break it. They laid her on the bed, and Mrs Marble wailed and dabbed at her eyes with her handkerchief which she still held clutched in her hand. John looked once more at his father, with a flash of hatred still in his eyes, and then he swung round and walked out of the room.

Perhaps even then all might have been well if Mr Marble had bent over his wife and had asked her pardon, in the little soft voice that he had sometimes used, which Annie loved so well. Annie might have softened; with her arms about his neck she might have pulled him down to her, and her broken-hearted tears might have changed to tears of joy even at that late moment. But Mr Marble did not do this. He was badly flustered and shaken; he stepped back from the bed and fidgeted round the room. When at last he came back to her Annie had her face buried in the pillow, and she shook off the hand he tentatively rested on her shoulder. Mr Marble dallied for a moment, but before his mind's eye rose a vision of a little drain of whisky left in the decanter downstairs. There was still a little left; he had seen it with his own eyes after Annie had picked up the decanter from where she had knocked it. And whisky at that moment was what Marble needed more than anything else in the world. He turned and tiptoed out of the room, downstairs to where the decanter was.

Late that night Mr Marble still sat in the drawing-room; he had lighted the gas, because he did not like the darkness he had found down there. His hand gripped an empty glass, and his eyes stared across the room as he sat in the armchair, faintly visualizing the sequence of events his over-active mind was tracing out. Too little whisky and too much excitement had stimulated Mr Marble's brain to such an extent that he could not check his wild imagination at all. The consequences of the evening's work were presented to him in every possible variation. At one second he seemed to feel the hands of the police on his shoulders; the next, and he could feel the hangman's slimy fingers upon him as they writhed over him making all ready. More than once he started from his chair mouthing a stream of inarticulate entreaties. Each time he sank back with a sigh, only to be plunged immediately afterwards into some other horrible fantasy. He had cut the ground from under his feet; he had made the blunder that every murderer had to make. His secret was shared, and a secret shared was a secret divulged. That fool Annie would never bear the strain he felt so hard. She would let fall something and then— the ghastly fancies recommenced. What Mr Marble needed was whisky, quantities of it, so that he could drown all these maddening thoughts. But whisky was just what Mr Marble could not have. Not all his twenty-seven thousand pounds, no, not all the wealth imaginable could buy whisky for Mr Marble at that time. In London it might have done, but not in that quiet suburb, at one o'clock in the morning. Mr Marble could only sit yammering in his chair, tormented to madness.

CHAPTER VII

MR MARBLE was, of course, deceiving himself when he imagined that his wife could deduce all that had happened from his half-hearted exclamations that night. He realized this as time passed. She could do nothing of the sort. The situation between them was still strained; they said as little to each other as they could help, but it was not because Annie knew her husband for a murderer. Mr Marble gradually regained his peace of mind in that respect.

And other things were too exciting for him to brood over it just at present. As he had expected, Mr Saunders had been unable to keep to himself the glorious fact that he had brought off a hundred to one success and had acquired the highly respectable sum of twenty-four thousand pounds. In two days the news was all over the City, and in three it had been brought to the official notice of the Bank. There had been a slight scene, in which Mr Marble bore himself with the arrogance only to be expected of a man with a fortune at his back. The Bank suspected the worst; told him more in sorrow than in anger that they would not prosecute this time—they had had no case anyway, and furthermore they would not expose their office routine to comment in a court of law —and then accepted the resignation that he tendered with a sigh of relief.

Yet Mr Marble did not become at once a gentleman of leisure. A distinguished firm of foreign exchange brokers heard Saunders' story and decided that a man of Mr Marble's talents would be a desirable acquisition. The only man in all the City who had foreseen the rise of the franc, who had had the courage of his convictions to put all his savings into the speculation, and who, besides, had the force of character to inveigle Saunders into supporting him would be a man worth having. So they approached Mr Marble, and made him a tentative offer which with little debate—he already had a vague idea that the more his thoughts were occupied the better—he accepted. The hours were easy; the junior partner was a little hesitant in mentioning the amount of the salary —five hundred a year. So Mr Marble found himself in a comfortable position with no less an income than seventeen hundred pounds a year. He struggled hard to stop himself from thinking about the fact that all this splendour was entirely due to the fierce stimulus of being in danger of the gallows.

The freehold of 53 Malcolm Road was safely purchased. It was only a matter of three days' negotiations, for the owners were overjoyed to find someone willing to pay seven hundred pounds for a house which cost twenty pounds a year in repairs and yet was not allowed by law to be rented at a greater sum than thirty-five pounds.

Mr Marble could afford to live in a house three times as expensive. But he could not bring himself to leave the place. He could not bear the idea of taking his eyes from that garden. Besides, he had a vague apprehension that there might be legislation compelling all owners of unoccupied houses to let them, and then the state of affairs which his tortured imagination so constantly pictured would naturally develop. No, he could not bear to leave the place, and so Mr Marble, with an income of seventeen hundred a year, continued to live in a shabby street, in a house with two tiny sitting-rooms, three tiny bedrooms, and a kitchen whose size Mrs Marble deplored every time she entered it.

Poor Annie Marble! She could hardly realize all the changes that would take place. The first convincing proof that matters were radically different occurred in a week or two after that unpleasant evening in the drawing-room. Mr Marble was leaving for town—he did not have to start until past nine o'clock nowadays—and as he said good-bye at the door he reached into his pocket and thrust something roughly into her hand.

'Here,' he said, 'take this and go out this morning and spend it, every bit of it. Mind you spent it all. There, good-bye.'

He dashed off up the road. Mrs Marble looked wonderingly at what he had given her. It was a roll of notes, crisp and fresh from the Bank. She passed them through her fingers. Some were five-pound notes, and some were one-pound notes. Altogether they amounted to an enormous sum—fifty pounds in all, actually—and it was more money than she had ever seen together at one time. Mr Marble, in the bus on the way to the station, felt a good deal more comfortable than he had done for the last two weeks. It had been rotten, not daring to meet his wife's eyes. She had a thin time, poor thing, and Mr Marble knew from experience that one of the few slight pleasures in her life was being able to spend money. With fifty pounds in her purse she would be able to go down Rye Lane and have a high old time. Perhaps when he came back that evening she would be smiling again and all that beastly business when he had lost control of himself would be forgotten.

But even while he was thinking this Mrs Marble was turning those notes over with fear in her heart. At that time her husband would have given her more pleasure by an unexpected gift of five shillings. For five shillings does not set one thinking of police and prisons. Besides, Mrs Marble hardly knew what to do with fifty pounds, and lastly she had too great a fear for the future to spend it all at once. Muddle-headed she may have been, but in her life Mrs Marble had learned one lesson, and that very thoroughly; it was to the effect that there is nothing as nice as money, nothing that goes so quickly, and nothing that is so hard to obtain. Mrs Marble went and locked it into the one private drawer she had in all the house.

She went slowly through her morning's work—she still had no help—making the beds, turning out one room, peeling potatoes for the children's dinner, and then she put her hat on to do her usual day's shopping. In the hall she hesitated for a moment, and then she yielded. Hurrying upstairs, she unlocked the drawer and guiltily peeled off one single pound note and thrust it into her purse.

Mr Marble returned home in time to join his children at their tea. As he came in he was obviously in good spirits, and Mrs Marble brightened as she saw that this all-too-rare mood was on him. Mr Marble looked round the room inquiringly; he put his head out into the hall again and peered up and down it. Then with much elaboration he began to search under the table and in all sorts of impossible places.

'What *are* you looking for, Will?' asked Mrs Marble. She could hardly help laughing at his antics.

'I'm looking for all the things you bought to-day,' was the reply.

Mrs Marble looked guiltily at her husband.

'With that money you gave me this morning?' she asked.

'That's right. I gave it to you to spend.'

'I didn't like to spend it all, dear. I only used a little of it.'

Mr Marble took a gold cigarette case out of his pocket, chose a gold-tipped cigarette, lighted it with a match from a gold matchbox, and looked across at her with half-concealed amusement.

'Well, what *did* you buy, then? Come on, let's hear all about it.'

Mrs Marble fumbled nervously with her dress.

'I—I bought one or two little things for the kitchen——'

'What were they?'

'A—a mop, dear, and two new pie-dishes——'

Mr Marble yelled with laughter.

'Splendid!' he said. 'And what else?'

'A new china pot for the aspidistra, such a nice one, dear, but, of course, they're sending that. And a wing for my other hat, the black one, you know. And—and— I don't think there's anything else. Oh, don't laugh like that. I couldn't help it.'

But Mr Marble only laughed the more. He rocked with merriment.

He turned to the children, and gasped out between his outbursts, 'I give your mother fifty pounds to go out and spend, and that's what she does with it! A mop and some pie-dishes! Oh, Annie, you'll be the death of me one of these days.'

Even the children realized that it was vague bad taste on his part to hold their mother up to ridicule before them, and poor Mrs Marble grew more and more flustered.

'Oh, don't laugh, Will, don't. How was I to know that you really wanted me to spend all that?'

But Mr Marble did not continue the argument.

'To-morrow's Saturday,' he said, 'and I'm not going to the office. We'll go out together and then I'll show you how to spend the money I give you. What about it?'

'Oh, that would be nice, dear.'

Little Mrs Marble was happily flustered now. It was perhaps a year since she had been out with her husband; it was probably three since she had been north of the Thames with him.

And yet that morning to which she looked forward so happily through the night was not wholly successful.

It was rather like a wild nightmare. They began in Tottenham Court Road at ten o'clock in the morning. Mr Marble began by making arrangements for having 'some old furniture' removed from 53 Malcolm Road. Then he began an orgy of buying. Clearly he was acting on some already-matured plan of his own, for he went straight to the 'period rooms' to make his purchases. But he did not want modest Queen Anne or beautiful Chippendale. That sort of thing was not in his line. Instead, he demanded Empire furniture. They gave it to him. In addition they gave him furniture of the period following close after the Empire, massively gilt, and showing evident traces of the debasement of taste that flooded the world from the forties onward. He bought over-gilded, over-florid chairs and couches. He bought an unsightly Empire bed ornamented with gilt Cupids in hideous taste. His crowning purchase was a massive table, the frame carved and chased and tortured into a monstrosity of design and then flamingly gilded; the body of the table was of marble mosaic, crudely arranged in feeble classical design. That table probably weighed between nine and ten hundredweight, and it looked like it.

The manager of the department rubbed his hands as the bargain was concluded. He could not remember a morning like this since the palmy days of the war. He foisted a few more white elephants on to Mr Marble, and then led them off in the direction of pictures and picture-frames. And yet that manager did not feel altogether happy while making these arrangements. The business was too simple. It was too like taking advantage of the feeble-minded. He had only to offer the thing, name its price, and book the order. Even he, skilled as he was in the mentality of the furniture-buyer, did not appreciate the fact that Mr Marble was buying what he wanted to buy, not what the manager wanted him to buy. Mr Marble was thoroughly enjoying himself. Those vast expanses of gilt, those florid designs like nightmare Laocoöns, were to Mr Marble's mind the perfection of good taste. As for the mosaic table, he considered himself lucky to have got hold of that.

So rapidly did Mr Marble make his purchases, and so little did he confer with his wife, that in two hours the whole business was completed. Mr Marble signed a cheque that gave him possession of enough debased Empire furniture to fill 53 Malcolm Road to overflowing, and was bowed out of the shop by an amazed and delighted staff.

On the pavement Mr Marble consulted the gold octagon-shaped watch on his wrist and hailed a taxicab.

'Oh, Will,' murmured Mrs Marble in deprecating tones, but she got in.

'Bond Street,' snapped Mr Marble to the driver, and climbed in beside her.

Mrs Marble clung desperately to her husband's arm as they bowled along Oxford Street. She was half afraid lest he might suddenly disappear, as so frequently happens in fairy stories, and leave her alone in a taxicab—she had never been in one before—to find her way home and face the arrival of a houseful of Empire furniture without the support of his presence. Mr Marble made no objection to this public display of affection. He even pressed the timid arm that lay between his own and his side, thereby sending Mrs Marble into the seventh heaven of delight. She was vaguely reminded of their honeymoon.

They got down at Bond Street tube station, and began to walk slowly down, their eyes on the shop windows. Mrs Marble began to wonder what was going to happen next. She soon found out.

'Go in there,' said Mr Marble, stopping outside a shop.

Mrs Marble glanced at the windows. The one or two articles displayed there proved without a doubt that it was a shop for women, and also that it was a shop for women with plenty of money. She clung to her husband's arm more wildly than ever.

'Oh, I can't, Will, I can't. I—I don't like to.'

Mr Marble snorted with contempt.

'Get along with you,' he said. 'Go and buy what you want. Nine women out of ten would give their ears for the chance.'

'Oh, but, Will, I don't know what I want. Let's—let's go to Selfridge's or somewhere.'

Mr Marble announced his contempt for Selfridge's to all Bond Street.

'Women never do know what they want when they go into a shop. You go in. Just leave it to them. They'll do all the asking that's necessary once you get inside and they find out how much money you've got. You got your fifty all right?'

'Yes, dear.' Mrs Marble was sure of that. She had been clutching her handbag all the morning in terror lest she should lose it.

'Right. Here's another twenty. Put it away. Now in you go.'

Mrs Marble, in the grip of a blind terror that made her knees tremble, tottered into the shop. Mr Marble wandered thirstily away in search of a drink.

When he returned his wife was still inside, and he had to wait dismally for some time before she emerged, pale but firm, and with a strange joy at her heart. She could tell him little of what had happened—Mrs Marble was not clever at describing experiences—and it was hopeless for her to endeavour to enlighten him about the feeling of hopeless inferiority that she had felt when she saw the look on the assistant's face when she had to confess miserably to an address in the unenlightened suburbs south of the river, and of the condescension of the whole staff towards her, and of the unmoved fashion in which they had kindly relieved her of all her money and further allowed her to order a great deal more than she had been able to pay for. And how she had realized as soon as she was inside the door that her clothes were dowdy and that her hat, even with the new wing that she had bought the day before, was not, in the eyes of those aristocratic assistants, a hat at all. In fact, none of her clothes were even clothes in their eyes. She had realized in a blinding flash that these people mentally divided the world into the clothed and the unclothed, and to them she was on no higher plane than a naked savage. But she had made up for it.

'I'm afraid I've spent an awful lot of money, Will,' she said apologetically.

'Quite right, too,' said Mr Marble. 'They're sending the things, I suppose? Sure you gave 'em the right address? That's all right, then. Let's go home.'

And home they went, in a bus crowded with the Saturday morning rush, back to Malcolm Road. It was rather unfortunate that when they arrived there, at two o'clock, there was nothing ready for them to eat, and Mr Marble had to wait while his wife, with her brain swimming in a delirium of chiffons and serges, prepared a hurried and indigestive meal. The best thing they could have done was to have had their lunch out, but Mr Marble had hardly thought of that. His old obsession had gripped him again; he was moody while on the bus, without a word to spare for his wife; he had been very anxious to get home to see that no one was interfering with that precious garden of his. This panic fear was displaying a growing habit of suddenly developing.

CHAPTER VIII

Next week kept all Malcolm Road on tiptoe. Various rumours had been flying round about Mr Marble's suddenly acquired wealth, stating its amount and its manner of coming in twenty different ways. Yet there were still some sceptics, who refused to believe the evidence presented to them, and who scornfully declared that they would give credit to the rumours only when they were proved beyond all doubt. Why, only a few months back there had been similar rumours, when the Marbles started to pay off their bills and Mrs Marble had bought some new clothes. But in a short time they had been back to their old tricks again, owing money on all sides, while Mrs Marble had been going about as dowdy as any of them.

But this time the sceptics were confounded. At first the news had flown from lip to lip—'Number 53's moving out'. It looked like it, indeed. An empty furniture van stood outside, and men were moving furniture into it from Number 53. Everywhere, from upper windows behind curtains, housewives were watching the process. Some, overwhelmed with curiosity, put on their hats and went thither on hurriedly-composed errands of borrowing or restoring in order to have a word with Mrs Marble to find out what was really going on. But they retired baffled. Mrs Marble was in too great a state of hurry and bewilderment to give them any satisfaction at all. And, having retired, they were doomed to further mystification. For more vans drew up outside Number 53, and from these men began to bring other furniture and take it inside.

Truly the neighbours were baffled. They had heard

of people moving out before, and they had heard of people moving in. They knew of many cases where these two operations had been carried out as nearly simultaneously as might be. They had also heard, but more rarely, of people buying new furniture although they were not newly married. But the present process utterly confounded them. And the furniture that was arriving! Nothing half as splendid had ever been seen before in Malcolm Road. They saw the great Empire bed being carried in in sections, the gilding flaming in the daylight, and the Cupids, vapidly chubby, clustered upon it. The neighbours shook their heads sadly, and told each other that they thought that that bed could tell a tale or two if it wished. Then came chairs, and dressing-tables, and chests of drawers, all resplendent in gold, and covered thick with carving. There was little housework done in Malcolm Road that day. The housewives were too busy watching the new furniture being brought in to Number 53.

The work was still uncompleted late in the afternoon when Mr Marble returned from the office. It was nearly done, but the task that remained was the hardest of all. The men were busy arranging to get the vast mosaic table into the house. Mr Marble, with quite a pleasant bubble of excitement within him, flung down his hat and hastened out to superintend the handling of this, his chiefest treasure. He stood by the gate, hatless in the sunshine, giving useless and unheeded advice while the workmen toiled and sweated, handling the monstrosity. Mrs Marble had sunk down on one of the uncomfortable gilt chairs, quite tired out.

As Mr Marble stood on the pavement by his gate he felt a touch on his arm, and he looked round. She was a woman nearly of middle-age—no, hardly that, thought Mr Marble, but at any rate she gave an impression of ripe and luscious maturity. And she was dressed—oh, simply to perfection. She was dressed as Mr Marble sometimes vaguely wished his wife would dress. Despite her closely-fitting hat anyone could tell that she was auburn-haired, and her eyes were a rich brown and her complextion was splendid. She wore her clothes in a fashion only achieved by her countrywomen—she was French. The whole atmosphere her appearance conveyed was one of ripeness and perfection—over-ripeness, perhaps, but that was, if anything, an added attraction in Mr Marble's eyes.

'What lovely things you have got,' said this apparition. 'I have been looking at them for ever so long. Those beautiful chairs and that lovely bed! They remind me of what I have seen in the Louvre.'

Mr Marble was a little taken aback. He was unused to being addressed in the broad light of day by over-ripe and entirely delectable goddesses. But he was secretly pleased. It was a pleasant thing to have this long-coveted Empire furniture admired, especially by people of obvious good taste like this one. Mr Marble realized that the difficulty that the newcomer displayed in tackling the aspirate was not the one usually met with in Malcolm Road. He noted her as French, with a pleased appreciation of his own perspicacity, and his head positively swam as he looked at her and strove to make some reply. The unknown noted his embarrassment, was pleased, and went swiftly on as though she had not.

'You do not mind my looking at your nice things? No? I am very rude, I know, and I should not, but I could not help it. And now I have confessed, and I ought to have pardon. You do pardon me, eh?'

Mr Marble had not even yet recovered himself, and this charming little speech did nothing to assist in the process. He stammered out some banal phrase or other—the only intelligible word was 'charmed'—but somehow the newcomer soon put him at his ease and they were chatting away as though they had been friends for years. She greeted the appearance of the mosaic table with little shrieks of delight.

'Oh, how lovely!' she said. 'It is magnificent. You are a very lucky man, Mr ——?'

'Marble,' said Mr Marble.

Upstairs, three doors off, one woman said to another:

'The French dressmaker woman, you know, Madame Collins, she calls herself, has just got off with Mr Marble. Nice goings on, I call it, right in the street outside his front door, with beds and I-don't-know-what being carried past them. I wonder what Mrs Marble will have to say about *that*.'

'Nothing, I don't expect. She doesn't never have a word to say for herself. He treats her cruel, so I've heard.'

But Mr Marble for the moment cared nothing for tittle-tattling neighbours. He was too busy thinking of something nice to say to this wonderful woman. He was still talking to her when the table had at last been manoeuvred through the narrow hall door and the workmen were gathering in the background with a furtive lust for tips in their eyes. He paid them testily, and signed the forms they held out to him without even glancing over them. He did not want her to go away just yet, but for the life of him he did not see how he could possibly detain her. Then came his wife, and this, instead of spoiling everything, as he had feared, was the saving of the situation. He was not to know that Madame Collins' dearest wish at the moment was to scrape acquaintance with such obviously well-to-do people. She had noted the furniture, and she had noted Mr Marble's well-cut clothes, just obtained from the best tailor in the City, and his platinum wrist-watch bracelet and his gold cigarette case. They would be acquaintances worth having, she had decided. When Mrs Marble appeared she went effusively towards her.

'Oh, Mrs Marble,' she said, 'I 'ave just been talking to your 'usband about all your nice furniture. It is too lovely. You are a lucky woman to 'ave such nice things.'

Mrs Marble was as startled as her husband had been ten minutes ago. She glanced quaveringly at him, and took from him her cue of agreeableness.

'I'm glad you like them,' she said.

Mr Marble took his chance.

'Won't you come in?' he said. 'Then you could see them in the rooms. My wife could give you a cup of tea, too.'

'Thank you so much,' said Madame Collins, and she passed the threshold, in more senses than one. They passed into the dining-room. It was crammed unbearably with gilt chairs and the abominable mosaic table, whose tawdriness was accentuated by the faded flowered wall-paper and what was left of the dingy old furniture. With its glitter and glare the room looked like a cheap-jack jeweller's stall. Madame Collins looked grimly round, but she was very charming about it, and praised the effect so delicately that even pale little Mrs Marble flushed with pleasure. And she introduced herself in such a ladylike fashion that everybody felt happy instead of uncomfortable as they expected to feel.

They had tea with the silver tea-set on the gilt and mosaic table—a combination that annoyed Madame Collins' really sensitive eye extremely—and when she rose to take her leave Mrs Marble was almost sorry, tired though she was, and she eagerly accepted Madame Collins' invitation to call whenever she felt like it.

Madame Collins had been very tactful and had let them know all about her past and present circumstances, without being too obvious about it. They had gathered that she was French, of a very old and distinguished family ruined by the war—her father was actually a Normandy peasant—and she had married an English officer of vast talent but no money. Now they were struggling to make both ends meet, she with her dress-making and he with his music. She admitted with a shy laugh that he really tuned pianos, but that was not at all the work he was fitted for. He had great ideas about what he could do, and—so she said—she believed in them, too. To Mrs Marble she conveyed the impression of a devoted couple with a great future before them; to Mr Marble it did not seem as if the devotion were so pronounced. That goes to show what a clever woman Madame Collins was, even allowing for the fact that Mrs Marble was very tired, and so preoccupied with being ladylike and pouring out the tea that she missed the one or two flashing glances with which Madame Collins favoured Mr Marble from her warm, brown eyes.

And when she had gone, Mr Marble, with his money scorching a hole in his pocket, was so excited and pleased with his inner thoughts that for the time he had no care about anything else. His riotous imagination had, for the nonce, something to riot over other than the possibilities of detection, and he made the most of it. He dreamed away the evening very pleasantly. He was not even disturbed by the fact that John and Winnie found it difficult to do homework on the mosaic table in conse-quence of the raised gilt border; he had no care for Mrs Marble, who was patiently clearing up the confusion left by the men when they had brought the furniture, and who was toiling putting mattresses and sheets on the cupid-encumbered Empire bed in the front bedroom.

But he paid for this slight relaxation. He had to pay for it sooner or later of course, and as it happened this came about the next evening.

Mr Marble was sitting smoking in the glittering dining-room. He was still happy and peaceful; he ignored the discomfort of the Empire armchair in which he sat; in the hall stood a crate of books he had ordered that morning—crime books, mystery books, all the books he had seen advertised at the back of the limited selection available at the Public Library, and had coveted during his poverty—and when he felt like it he would leisurely unpack them and would arrange them in the drawing-room so that he could browse in them when he would. But he was rudely disturbed. Mrs. Marble had come into the room and had sat down, and was fidgeting with her sewing in a nervous fashion. If Mr Marble had given the matter a thought he would have known that she was nerving herself to ask something of him, but he had been too preoccupied in thinking about Madame Collins and her brown eyes—the money in his pocket had something to do with it as well—and the natural result was that her request took him unawares.

'Will,' said Mrs Marble, 'don't you think we could have Mrs Summers back here again now that we can afford it? This house means a lot of work for me, and now that we've got all this new furniture——'

Mr Marble sat very still. His mind had raced away to all the books about crimes that he had read. He had impressed it upon himself so very often that he could only be found out if he made some stupid mistake, like the people whose unhappy lives were told in *Historic Days at the Assizes*. He was not going to make any stupid mistake. Mrs Summers was a harmless soul enough, but she had the usual besetting sin of charwomen—inquisitiveness. Goodness knows what she might not find out for herself. Or perhaps his wife would say something that would set her tongue wagging in the other houses in which she worked. It was only to be expected. Mr Marble did not mind being gossiped about—he rather liked it, in the ordinary way, in fact. But he would have no gossip about himself nowadays. He simply could not afford it. He could foresee with vivid clearness what would happen. His wife would let fall a careless word or two, and Mrs Summers would repeat them equally carelessly but with a lavish percentage of imaginative detail. The woman who heard her would tell someone else, and before anyone could say Jack Robinson there would be all sorts of tales flying round. There was plenty of gossip about him already, thanks to the new furniture; any addition might result in disaster—anonymous letters to the police, or a committee of neighbours coming secretly to investigate. No one would know, of course, anything about the real state of affairs, but Mr Marble did not want there to be any suspicion, however baseless, attached to him. For his position was not absolutely secure. If the interest of the police were sufficiently roused even for them to make a casual inspection of all his financial arrangements they might easily find something to interest them regarding certain banknotes that had passed into his possession one stormy night last winter. And it was not mere money that was at stake, nor comfort, nor even Empire furniture. What was in peril was his life! Much reading of books about crime had given him a good idea of the formalities of the condemned cell and of the scaffold. And he writhed in anguish at the thought. He could not possibly run any risks. Already in imagination he was being torn from his bed one bleak morning, and dragged fainting along a grey corridor to a tarred shed wherein awaited him a trapdoor and a noose. There was sweat on his face as he forced this picture on one side and turned to face his wife.

'No,' he said, 'we don't want any charwomen in here. You will have to manage on your own.'

Even Mrs Marble expostulated at this arbitrary decision.

'But, Will, dear,' she said, 'I don't think you understand. I'm not asking for anything, I'm not really. You're giving me nine pounds a week housekeeping money, and that's a lot more than I can spend at all. We could have a maid to live in with all that money, two maids perhaps, with caps and aprons and all. But I don't want that. They'd be too much trouble. I only want old Mrs Summers to come in three or four days a week and help me with the rough work. It's too much for me, really and truly it is.'

'What, in this little house?'

'Of course I *could* do it, if I had to, Will. But it does seem silly, doesn't it, that I should have to sweep and dust and wash up, when there are lots of people who would be thankful to have the chance to do it for me? And my back still aches from lifting those mattresses yesterday.'

'Nonsense,' said Mr Marble.

Mrs Marble was incapable of sustaining an argument for long. She had already made two speeches, each of them thrice the length of any of her usual remarks, and she could do no more for the present. She relapsed into unhappy silence, while Mr Marble battled with the train of thought that had been raised by his wife's suggestion. His imagination tortured him with peculiar malignity for the next few minutes.

Mrs Marble's mind was working, too. That day had seen the arrival of the first of the things she had bought last Saturday—large boxes delivered by carrier, and full of the most delectable things her imagination had ever pictured. She had lingered over them lovingly. There were hats, wonderful hats, which suited her marvellously, although, as she confessed to herself, she did not much care for the fashionable cloche shape with its severely-untrimmed lines. There were jumpers, matronly jumpers, which she realized with amazement looked very well on her although up till then she had only considered jumpers as suitable for young girls. There were boxes and boxes of underclothing, whose price had horrified her at first, until she had taken heart of grace from the knowledge of all the money there was to spend. Naturally, she had not yet received the tailored costume and the coatfrock for which she had been measured by a woman's tailor who had appeared startlingly in the shop as she finished her other purchases—startlingly, that is to say, to Mrs Marble, unacquainted with the commission-sharing system of ladies' shops and with the conveniences of the telephone.

But that costume and the coatfrock would not have been any good to her even if she had had it. Mrs Marble had indeed roused herself to put on some of the underclothing, priceless things, warm and weightless, costing as much as her husband had earned in a month before all this started happening, but she had not the heart to put on a pair of the thick silk stockings while she had so much housework still to be done, and she wore over the wonderful underclothing her usual draggled housefrock. With the other things arriving shortly she might as well have put on her best frock, but she had not the heart to do that with so much washing-up to be done that evening. Mrs Marble felt aggrieved. Besides, she was tired, and her back really did hurt.

A day or two ago she had pictured herself sitting at her ease in the evenings, wearing a wonderful frock, with her skin deliciously thrilled by the contact of the silken underclothing. As it was, she wore a shabby frock and there was a bowlful of washing-up clamouring for her attention in the kitchen. It was this that roused her to surprising rebellion—very mild rebellion, but any sort of rebellion was surprising in Mrs Marble.

'I'll have Mrs Summers in during the daytime when you don't know anything about it,' she said.

The words brought Mr Marble out of his chair in a panic. That would be worse than the other thing; it would start gossip of a more poisonous sort than ever, and gossip better directed towards the real food for suspicion, for Mrs Marble would have to tell Mrs Summers that he did not like having other people about the house. He glared at her with frightful intensity.

'You mustn't, you mustn't ever do anything like that,' he said, and his voice was cracked and shrill. His clenched fists shook in his agitation. Mrs Marble could only stare at him, surprised and speechless.

'You mustn't do it. Do you hear me?' he shrieked.

His agitation infected his wife, and she fumbled nervously with the sewing on her lap.

'Yes, dear.'

'Yes, dear! Yes, dear! I don't want any of your "yes, dears". You must promise me, promise me faithfully, that you won't ever do that. If ever I find out, I'll—I'll——'

Mr Marble's high-pitched scream died away as the door swung open. John had come running down as soon as he heard his father's voice at that hysterical pitch. It was not very long since the last time he had heard it like that, and then he had had to carry his mother up to bed, and she had a bruise on her face.

John stood by the door with the light on his face. Mr Marble shrank back a little, and his lips wrinkled back from his teeth. He was the rat in the corner once more. Hatred flashed from the father to the son. It was not John's fault, nor, by that time, was it Mr Marble's. For James Medland, he who had come in that memorable evening, nearly a year ago now, was John's cousin when all was said and done, and there was a considerable family likeness. As John stood by the door he was in the same attitude and in the same light as Medland had been in, that evening, when he had entered the dining-room after Winnie had opened the door to him. No wonder that Mr Marble hated John, and had hated him ever since he first noticed the likeness, that evening when he had struck his wife.

Father looked at son, son looked at father. The room

was all aglare with gilded furniture. The diamond in
Mr Marble's tiepin winked and glittered as he shrank
slowly back before John's slow and menacing advance.
John had come to protect his mother, but the desperate
challenge in his father's attitude had roused him to the
limit of his self-control. It was Mrs Marble who saved
the situation. She glanced terror-stricken at her husband's
snarling countenance, and at the wrinkled scowl of her
son. In utter fear she flung herself into the breach.

'John, go away,' she said. 'Go—quickly—it's all right.'
John checked himself, and his hands unclenched. Mrs
Marble's hand was on her heart; for in that same second
she had seen what her husband had seen long before, and
she had guessed that it was this that had called up that
ferocity into his face. She was frightened, and she did
not yet know why.

'Go, go, go,' wailed Mrs Marble, and then, with a
supreme effort, 'There's nothing to worry about John.
You had better go to bed. Good night, sonny.'

When he had gone, silent, wordless as when he had
entered, Mrs Marble sank into a chair and laid her face
on her arms on the gilded table and sobbed and sobbed,
heartbroken, while her husband stood morosely beside
her, hands in pockets, the gaudy glare of the ornate
furniture mocking him, mocking his hopes of the future,
mocking his submerged, sensual dreamings of Madame
Collins.

CHAPTER IX

AFTER this episode matters went for some time exactly as Mr Marble would have wished. John's application to enter Sydenham College was favourably received, and he went there without further demur. He was not quite sixteen. There was more trouble about Winnie. Mr Marble obtained from scholastic agents a list of all the more expensive girls' schools, but his endeavours to enter Winnie in one of them were baulked for some time. They displayed a not unnatural reluctance to receive in their midst a girl of nearly fifteen who hailed from an address in a dubious street in a south London suburb, and who had been educated so far at a Council school and at a secondary school. But at last a Berkshire school accepted her—it was incidentally the most expensive of all—and then there was a flurrying and a scurrying to get ready the vast outfit that the rules of the school demanded. There was a special type of gymnasium frock to be obtained, and day clothes and evening clothes and, crowning glory of all, a riding-habit and boots. Mr Marble was delighted. He certainly seemed prouder of Winnie's outfit than she was herself.

And so, after Easter, the same day that Mr and Mrs Marble, he dressed in his very best to impress the other girls' parents and the other girls, she rather tearful, with her appearance not justifying the amount spent on it, saw Winnie off from Paddington, John put on the blue and black cap of Sydenham College and set off on his two-mile walk thither, not feeling at all happy, with all the mysteries of Rugby football and the prevailing etiquette of the new school before him.

True, his father had been jolly decent to him lately.

He had given him nearly all the pocket-money he wanted, while in a tiny lock-up garage at the end of Malcolm Road there reposed the giant two-cylinder motor-bicycle that his heart had yearned for. John had averaged a hundred miles a day on it for the last week, delighting in learning its mechanical whims, making gallant and occasionally successful attempts to climb hills in 'top', and finding all the wonderful bits of country that lie near London just out of reach of the ordinary bicycle. It was a good way of forgetting saying good-bye to the old school, where he had been happy for nearly five years— and saying good-bye to his old friends, too.

John was violently unhappy. It was not altogether the new school that made him so, not by any means. It was affairs at home. His father was drunk five nights out of seven, and that was the least of his troubles. Most times Mr Marble's drunkenness did not disturb the rest of the family as much as might be expected, for on those occasions he kept himself very strictly to himself—shut up in the drawing-room gazing out over the backyard. Only twice had John to interfere actively between his mother and his father, fearing that he would do her an injury, but John knew in his soul that there was a far worse trouble than drunkenness in his house. His mother was looking pinched and thin, and he guessed repeatedly that she had been crying during the day. His father's unaccountable moroseness probably caused that, combined with the fatigue resulting from his unreasonable refusal to allow her to have any help about the house. Yet John could not find any definite beginning to this moroseness and cross-grainedness, for Mr Marble had drunk more than was good for him and had neglected his wife long before James Medland had made his solitary visit to 53 Malcolm Road. John looked upon the unpleasing traits in his father's character as plants of slow growth and poisonous flowering.

All John knew was that there was trouble in the family, terrible trouble, too, and he guessed, childlike, at his father's hatred for him and resented it with a hatred equally bitter. The gifts that his father had showered on him so profusely lately he had accepted because there was hardly any other course open to him; and he had offered no thanks, because he had seen that what Mr Marble desired more than anything was to dazzle him with his profusion, and—somewhere—there was a lurking suspicion that these gifts were a sort of bribe, offered to keep him in a good temper.

But at fifteen—nearly sixteen—John had not thought out all these things in the clear-cut fashion of print. He still thought child fashion, all instinct and intuition, but that did not make him any the less unhappy. In fact, it tended rather in the contrary direction.

It was hardly surprising that during that term John found himself very much to himself, and that his already well-developed taste for being solitary increased under stress of circumstances. At school he was that most uncomfortable of beings, the old new boy. The thirteen-year-old at a new school enters a low form, where he finds others of his kind with whom to congregate; he is not expected to know the little points of etiquette that are so vastly important; friends come to him automatically. But John found himself in the Remove, only one form below the Sixth. The others in his form had long ago formed their own particular sets and cliques, and not one of them had room for John. They had been at no pains to conceal their amusement at the one or two blunders into which he unwittingly fell, and, if the truth must be told, their opinion of him was not increased by the knowledge that he had come from the secondary school a mile away for which they had an unreasoning contempt. John resented their attitude towards him, resented it bitterly, and was unwise enough to show it.

That raised the baiting of 'young Marble' in the eyes of his schoolfellows from the level of a pastime to that of a duty. His very name, of course, gave them endless opportunities for being witty. It ended, as was inevitable, in John's flinging away from them in disgust, thanking God he was a day boy, and only coming into contact with his fellows when the elastic rules of compulsory games compelled him to.

But unhappily it was just as bad with the fellows with whom he had been friendly at the other school. He went to some pains to look them up and to keep in touch with them, but he was soon conscious of how far they had fallen apart. There was just a trace of suspicion in their attitude towards him—they were always ready to note, and resent, any hint of condescension on his part. Their holidays were different now, for the secondary school had all day on Saturday free, while John was at school in the morning, receiving Wednesday afternoon instead, and the long excursions they were in the habit of making could not be cut down by half to allow him to join them. Besides, did he not have a motor-bicycle, so that he would see no point in sweating with them on a push-bike? And in honest truth John soon found that the savour had gone out of pedal-cycling now that he knew the joys of forty miles an hour on the Giant Twin. Once or twice, at John's urgent invitation, they had come to 53 Malcolm Road, but John had found himself regretting the invitation as soon as it had been accepted. Those rooms full of gaudy furniture did not make them feel at home. Mr Marble had been barely civil to them, and had made obvious the fact that he was not entirely sober; John, desperately sensitive, had suspected them of finding much to joke about among themselves at the Marble *ménage*, and had hated himself for his disloyalty at thinking them capable of such a thing and yet had still gone on thinking it.

All things considered, it was as well that John had the consolation offered him by the Giant Twin. That bulky machine became as good as a brother to him, sharing his troubles and giving him, in the very few mechanical defects it developed, other things to think about than the drunkenness of his father and the disorder of his home.

It is only doing Mr Marble bare justice to admit that he was happily unconscious of the turmoil in his son's life. He had other things to think about, too, matters of life and death. The old obsessions were gripping him hard, despite all the distractions offered him in the fact of his having a son at the College, and a daughter at the most expensive school in Berkshire, and a new interest in his life centring in a house in the next road whose gate was adorned with a brass plate bearing the legend 'Madame Collins, Modes and Robes'. The evenings were many when the lure of that house was not sufficient to drag him away from his steady watching over the back-yard from his coign of vantage in the drawing-room.

Marble had more to lose now: security of income, a house full of Empire furniture, a rapidly-expanding and catholic library of books on criminal matters, as much whisky as he was able to drink, a woman who took a more than friendly interest in him. And the irony of it lay in the fact that the more he had to lose the more anxious he was not to lose it, and the more difficult it became in consequence to enjoy all these priceless possessions. Those summer months fled past him like a maelstrom; he was hardly conscious of what was happening around him. The sweets of life were bitter to his palate, in that they were poisoned by the girding worry that was ever present and ever increasing.

The summer term flashed by. It hardly seemed a week since he had seen Winnie off from Paddington before his wife began to make arrangements for her return. Then she spoke to Mr Marble about holidays.

'Holidays,' said Mr Marble, vaguely.

'Yes, dear. We're going away this summer, aren't we?'

'I don't know,' said Mr Marble. 'Are we?'

'We didn't go away at all last summer,' said Mrs Marble, 'and the one before that we only had those few days at Worthing. We can afford it, can't we?'

'M'yes. I suppose so. But I don't know what arrangements the office are making.'

'Oh, dear,' said Mrs Marble. She had looked forward to a holiday this year, if only to get away from having to look after that house and to give her a chance of wearing all the wonderful clothes she had bought.

'I suppose you had better go anyway,' said Mr Marble, who was absolutely determined that he, for one, was not going to leave that house unguarded. 'I'll look up some nice hotel for you and the kids to go to. I might come down for a bit if I can get away from the office.'

Annie Marble drew her breath in sharply. A hotel! No washing-up, no bother about food, servants to do her bidding; it seemed like a prospect of heaven. There was just a slight momentary fear in her bosom as she thought of possible motives in Mr Marble's handsome offer, but her suspicions were too unformed for her to be very worried, and further, there were two possible motives for Mr Marble wishing to be left in the house, and Mrs Marble was a little too muddleheaded to disentangle them. Instead, she accepted gratefully.

'But are you sure you'll be all right, dear?' she said, perforce.

'Of course I will.' And that settled the matter.

Soon after Winnie came back from school, strangely mature, and rapidly fulfilling her early promise of beauty. She seemed a different girl, somehow. There was an alteration in her speech. Not that she had ever talked broad cockney—her other school friends had always considered her 'refined', but the slight trace of a twang when she used the higher registers had now disappeared, in fact, she did not employ those higher registers at all now. She talked more throatily—'pound-notey' was the terse descriptive phrase popular in that district—and she was much more self-possessed and placid than she had been when she went away. Mr Marble was pleased, as pleased as he could be at that period—he was going through rather a bad time just then—and Mrs Marble, as was inevitable, was heartily sorry. Winnie had grown away from her.

But neither of her parents, much as they fussed about her when she arrived, noticed her tiny lift of the eyebrows as she entered their wonderful dining-room, with its wonderful mosaic table. Winnie had now had experience of what good rooms look like, and to her, the half-forgotten gaudiness of the gilt furniture in terrible contrast to the faded wallpaper was indescribably vulgar.

Later she hinted as much to her mother, but her comments were not received very gratefully. Mrs Marble at once began to fidget with her sewing—a sure sign that she was embarrassed.

'Your father has one or two odd fancies, dear,' she said, fumbling, blushing and stammering. 'I shouldn't mention it to him if I were you. He doesn't like the idea of having a lot of people about the house, as we should have to have if we had any decorations done. Besides,'—she bridled a little, for she was as proud as was her husband of the gilt furniture.—'I'm sure this room looks very well indeed. I'm sure nobody in this road has anything half as good in their house. I don't expect there are many rooms like this in London, even. And, of course, every room in the house is done in the same way. Madame Collins says it's as good as the Louvre, and she ought to know, seeing she's been there.'

And that at once placed the matter beyond argument,

for Madame Collins was by now a great friend of the family's. But Winnie would not have argued about it, anyway. She merely made a mental note of the fact and said no more about it. That was typical of Winnie.

But Mrs Marble had by now become well started on the subject that absorbed so many of her few thoughts.

'You mustn't think any the less of your father, dear, because—because—he is a little odd at times. He has a great deal to worry him, you know, and I'm sure you ought to be grateful to him for all he's done.'

'Of course I am,' said Winnie, sweetly. It had never occurred to her to be grateful.

'I'm so glad. I—I was a little afraid that when you came back from your fine school you might find that—that—everything was not quite as you would like it.'

'Do you mean because father drinks?'

'Winnie!' Mrs Marble showed in her expression how shocked she was at this calling of a spade a spade.

'But he does, mother, now doesn't he?'

'Y—es, I suppose he does. But not very much, dear. Not more than you could expect, seeing how much his business worries him. And you didn't ought to speak about it like that, Winnie. It doesn't sound nice.'

Poor Mrs Marble had by now nearly as much to worry her as her husband had. It might almost be worse in her case, for she did not know really what it was she had to worry about, and her not over-exuberant imagination could not allow her even to guess. And the worry of defending her husband to her children on unnamed and unguessed-at charges was nearly as great as everything else put together.

For her children were small comfort to her now. John was gawky and shy, and she could not know of the love he bore her, especially as the memory of the times when he had come to defend her from her husband stood as a barrier between them which neither of them had the

moral courage to surmount at a rush. And Winnie—
even Mrs Marble felt this—was just a little bit *superior*
nowadays.

Yet even Winnie was for the moment mollified by the
announcement that they were going to stay for a month
at the Grand Pavilion Hotel at a very fashionable south
coast resort. That would be much nicer than staying all
the holidays at Malcolm Road, and it would be something to tell the girls about when she went back to
school. Some of these might go to France, some to Italy,
but there would be few who would spend their holidays
at such a place as the Grand Pavilion Hotel. Their
parents would have more sense.

And the packing, and the preparation! Winnie helped
her mother sort out her astonishing wardrobe. In the tiny
cupboards of the bedroom upstairs, where the gilt cupids
climbed eternally about the big bed, there were heaps of
the most assorted clothes it was possible to conceive.
Mingled with the frightfully expensive costumes, there
were old rags dating back from the dark ages before the
rise of the franc. Mrs Marble, apparently, wore indifferently the pastel shade silk underclothes bought in Bond
Street and the wool and cotton mixture garments, neither
decorative nor useful, which she had had before the
arrival of these others. The explanation was really simple.
Never in her life before had Mrs Marble had any clothes
to give away; they were all worn to rags long before she
could spare them. She could not get into the habit of
disposing of her older wardrobe. In fact, it is much to be
doubted whether she had ever contemplated giving away
garments in which there still remained six months' wear,
according to earlier standards of economy. And all the
clothes, worn and unworn, were badly looked after, un-
brushed and hung on hooks without hangers.

Even one term at a boarding-school had taught Winnie
to do better than this, and for two hectic days she took

her mother's clothes in hand, sorting and folding, ruthlessly relegating some to the rag-basket, wondering over others. It was beyond her powers to imagine her mother in underclothing of orange silk or *eau de nil*; it was almost beyond it to imagine her well dressed at all, but Winnie contrived to arrange that her mother looked more like the mothers whom she had seen at the school occasionally. Mrs Marble was almost tearfully grateful.

'I don't seem to have time to do all this,' she said. 'And —and—it doesn't seem worth it, sometimes. Your father is a very busy man, you know, dear.'

The cupids that climbed about the big Empire bed had climbed in vain for months now, that was what Mrs Marble implied, although she would never have dreamed of hinting as much to her daughter.

And in all this rush to put Mrs Marble's wardrobe in order Winnie herself was not forgotten. She had to have new frocks as well, for her stay at the Grand Pavilion Hotel, and Winnie's taste, which was allowed almost complete freedom, was at its best a little juvenile. Mrs Marble was a shade frightened when she saw some of the things Winnie had chosen, but it was beyond her to protest. She had only the haziest idea as to what was the correct wear for a girl of fifteen at the Grand Pavilion Hotel.

'There's a lot in being bobbed,' said Winnie to herself in the glass, attentively studying her features while her mother was safely out of the way. 'No one can ever really tell how old you are. If I weren't bobbed, I wouldn't have my hair up, and then anyone could tell. But as it is, with my new frocks and everything, I think I'll have rather a nice time this holiday. And there'll be something to tell them about when I get back to school.'

Winnie and her mother were pleasantly excited when the cab came to take them to Victoria. John was not with them. He had decided to go on alone on the Giant Twin, despite Winnie's faint protest that a motor-bicycle was highly vulgar.

Mr Marble, too, was pleasantly excited when he waved good-bye to them. For reasons of his own he was glad to know that his daughter was out of the way. He had felt uncomfortable in her presence. That three months, three months of good food and of close intimacy with people who never had the slightest difficulty with their aitches, had caused her to grow away from her family at a surprising rate. Mr Marble was not even comfortable with his daughter when he was drunk. And every moment he feared lest she should demand that they should move to a bigger and better house, or failing that, that they should have the present house redecorated and arranged as nearly as possible like the houses of the girls she had known at school. It was not the expense that Mr Marble feared. Instead, he was thrown into agonies of terror at the thought of workmen nosing around his house, and of piles of ladders and boards heaped up in his backyard. The foot of a ladder might easily dig some inches deep into the soft soil of the barren flower-bed.

When he was sober, Mr Marble had his suspicions, too, that his children were neither grateful for nor impressed by the benefit he had heaped upon them. He even suspected them of not admiring the mosaic table as much as they should have done. In a ferment of self-pity he realized that he was not getting full return for all his outlay. When he could blame it on to circumstances he did not mind so much; but there were a few aching moments, when the whisky had failed to bite as it should, when it was forced home on him that it was his fault. There were times when he could not visualize himself, as he usually could, as the triumphant criminal, surmounting all difficulties, over-riding all obstacles, tearing success out of the very teeth of failure. Instead, there came moments when he saw himself in his true colours, as the cornered rat he was, struggling with the courage of desperation against the fate that would inevitably close upon him sooner or later. When these black periods came he would clutch hurriedly at his glass and drain it thirstily. Thank God, there was always whisky in exchange for his money—and Marguerite Collins.

CHAPTER X

MADAME COLLINS was a highly successful intriguer, now that she had gained experience and the poise given by experience. To no one in the suburbs, not even to the milk roundsman, is given the opportunity for gossip which the suburban dressmaker enjoys. After the costume has been fitted, and changing naturally from the easy and fertile subject of clothes, there comes a time in every interview with every customer when local affairs must be discussed. Some merely talk parish shop, and with these Madame Collins had to walk warily, but most are only too willing to discuss neighbours, especially to a sympathetic audience of one, and that a woman. Madame Collins heard all about Mr Marble's newly acquired wealth almost as soon as he acquired it. She had noted the information mentally; rich men were always desirable acquaintances, especially to a woman utterly wearied of life in a suburb on very little money after the varied experiences she had enjoyed as a girl in a district occupied by English troops during the war.

The historic meeting with Mr Marble on the day that

the furniture arrived was only partly planned. Madame Collins had been walking along Malcolm Road on perfectly legitimate business when she had seen all the massy gilt being carried in, and she had been impressed. They must have cost a great deal of money, even if they were in abominable taste, and then when she had seen Mr Marble himself, tie-pin, wrist-watch, cigarette case, well-cut clothes and all, her mind was at once made up. There must be a great deal of truth in what she had heard about his money. It was the easiest thing in the world to scrape acquaintance with him after that.

Then in a week's time what Madame Collins did not know about the Marble *ménage* was hardly worth knowing—save for the, to her, unimportant detail about a certain transaction consummated twenty months before in the Marbles' dining-room. Neighbours had already hinted that all was not well between Mr Marble and his wife, and that was all the knowledge Madame Collins asked for. A rich man estranged from his wife, and that wife simple enough to be easily hoodwinked, living conveniently near, meant all the colour and all the money that Madame Collins' drab life demanded—especially seeing that he was obviously a raw hand in dealings with women, and had not yet had his money long enough to be spoilt by it.

To Mrs Marble, Marguerite Collins had borne Greek gifts. She had offered her a friendship which the lonely woman had eagerly accepted. She had invited her to her little house in the next street, and there had introduced her to her husband, proving that she was a perfectly respectable married woman. Annie Marble did not appreciate what a cipher Collins himself was.

For Collins was a dull and a tragic figure. He was cursed with an intense sensitiveness for music combined with complete absence of creative talent. All his life, with the exception of a violent interval in France during the last year of the war culminating in his marriage to Marguerite, he had earned his living tuning pianos. He was a very good piano tuner, and highly prized by the firm that employed him. Therein lay the tragedy. For the perfect piano tuner must never play the piano. If he does, he loses half his worth as a tuner. His ear loses that shade of anxious accuracy that makes him the perfect tuner. So Collins, thirsty for music, inexpressibly moved by music, spent his life in a piano factory tuning pianos, eternally tuning pianos. No wonder that Marguerite Collins found life drab.

Collins accepted the advent of the Marbles into his wife's life with the lack of interest that he evinced towards everything. He talked with weary politeness to Marble himself on the one or two occasions that the latter had accompanied Annie there. But he probably did not know their names. After all these years of married life he had ceased to be interested in his wife's doings. Marguerite, red-haired, brown-eyed, tempestuously passionate, and with her native peasant craftiness to guide her, was by no means the ideal wife for him. By that time they both knew it.

Marguerite played her new capture with dexterous skill—not that there was much skill needed, seeing that Marble's greatest wish at the moment was to be her captive, provided no one else knew about it. There had been glances from her hot brown eyes into which Mr Marble was at liberty to weave all sorts of meanings. There had been strange coincidences when she had happened to be out shopping just when Mr Marble was walking home from the bus that brought him from the station. There had been times, anxiously awaited, when he had escorted her home after she had been to Malcolm Road calling in the evening. Then, in the comforting darkness, she had walked close at his side so that he could feel her warmth against his. She had long ago decided that she would yield to him, but she was not going to yield too readily. She wanted money as well as intrigue, money that she could put into the bank account that stood in her name alone, in which her husband had no share. Peasant avarice was in her blood, the avarice that demands hard money and plenty of it—enough too, to enable her to forsake her spiritless husband and live her own life in Rouen or even Paris.

But she nearly miscalculated, owing to her not being in possesion of all the data. There came a time when in place of the pleasant lunches in town—when she had to be up buying her materials—a little dinner was suggested. Marguerite had the whole scene in her mind's eye. There would be a private room, and a discreet waiter, and plenty of good wine—Burgundy, she thought would be best. Then, with Mr Marble well warmed and comforted, would come the tale of unexpected business losses and of pressing debts. Mr Marble might not believe it; he would be welcome not to. But he would offer a loan, nevertheless, and when she had it safely in her purse, she would melt with gratitude towards him. She would be overcome, yielding, tender. Then she would hear no more about that 'loan'. But the farce would be necessary, nevertheless. Otherwise Mr Marble might get unwelcome ideas into his head—that it was solely by his charms that he had overcome her resistance. Marguerite preferred to have matters on a sound business footing.

At first everything went according to plan. Marguerite arrived only ten minutes late, just enough to make Mr Marble anxious and yet not long enough seriously to annoy him. And at the sight of her all anxiety vanished. She was in splendid evening dress, low-cut and dazzling, so that Mr Marble caught his breath as he looked at her. He himself was in a lounge suit, as was necessary with a wife at home who would look for some explanation should he do anything so extraordinary as to go out in dress clothes.

There had been no difficulty about obtaining a room to themselves; the waiter had been discreet, the wine had been good, the dinner excellent. Marguerite noted with pleasure that Marble ate hardly anything. He seemed to be in a fever.

Marble sat at the table. He was paying no attention to the woman opposite him. Coffee and liqueur brandy stood awaiting his leisure. The waiter had gone for good, with his bill paid. Marguerite was about to bring her carefully-rehearsed story into action, when she noticed the look on his face. He was staring, staring hard, past her at the opposite wall. In that direction lay the door that led into the tawdry bedroom, but clearly he was not thinking about that. The stare was a stare of agony.

Marble had felt uneasy almost as soon as the arrival of Madame Collins had set free his thoughts to wander where they would. He had a sudden awful suspicion that while he was dallying here someone was interfering with the flower-bed in his backyard. It would be poetic justice if it were so—newspaper poetic justice. He could imagine their baldly moral comments in the flaming reports that would appear in the next day's papers. Cases of that kind, where there had been long concealment of the body, were nearly as popular in the newspapers as cases where the body had been cut up or burnt. And he would be dragged away. Then—his thoughts jumped back to half-remembered fragments of a stray copy of *The Ballad of Reading Gaol* which had come into his possession. There was something about 'the black dock's dreadful pen'. His mind hovered there for a space, and then fled on through all the horrible verses about 'the silent men who watch him night and day' and about crossing his own coffin as he moves into the hideous shed. Then writhing into his mind came the lines about having a cloth upon his face and a noose about his neck. Marble's breath came croakingly through his dry, parted lips. In imagination he already had a cloth upon his face. He could feel it, stifling, blinding him, while the officials padded warily about him making all ready. Marble struggled in his chair.

Madame Collins' voice came to him, apparently from an immense distance, asking him if he were ill. Even then he only came partially to himself. At her anxious questionings he only laughed. Annie Marble had heard laughter like that once in her life. It was a mirthless sound, a disgusting sound. Marguerite shrank back in horror, crossing herself. Marble's chair scraped hideously as he dragged himself up from the table.

'Home,' he said, leaning first on the table, then on her shoulder, for support, 'home, quickly.'

Downstairs they went together, he with dragging steps yet striving to hasten, she with horror and fright in her eyes. They went home as fast as a taxicab could take them. Mr Marble's fears had, of course, been baseless. Not a soul had been in the backyard. But he could not explain to Marguerite Collins about the silly fright he had given himself. Nor, on the other hand, could he convince himself that his fears were unjustified. The obsession was growing. Mr Marble was experiencing more and more reluctance to spend his spare time anywhere whence he could not keep his eye on that backyard of his. And yet he lusted after Marguerite Collins of the warm hair as he lusted after little else. That was why he was so pleasantly excited to see his family drive off to Victoria on their way to the Grand Pavilion Hotel.

Marguerite was pleased, too. She was a woman of strong common sense, and rapidly recovered from the fright she had had.

For Marble began the happiest month he had known since James Medland's visit. There was no bothering family to worry him at all. He cooked his own breakfast after a fashion, and his other meals he had out save for the occasions when he bought cooked food and consumed it at home. The evenings were very long and pleasant at first. He could sit and brood in the drawing-room with a book about crimes on his knee, drinking as he wished, without the worried eyes of his wife to cause him annoyance, and even though sometimes his thoughts began to stray towards detection and failure he was able at that period to change them, in consequence of the new interest he had. For sometimes as it grew dark, there would come a hurried little tap at the door, and he would go and open it to Marguerite Collins. She would come in superb, wonderful, ripe to rottenness, and then Marble would forget his troubles entirely for the time. He did not appreciate her taste in wine, but he saw that there was always wine for her. For himself he was content with whisky, and the time would fly by. At the end of the evening there would be a passing of a little bundle of money—trust Marble to deal in cheques as little as possible under these circumstances—and Marguerite would slip out as quietly as she came.

They were strange evenings, half dream, half nightmare. By a queer twist of thought, Marble found that the sharing of his house and of its view of the backyard was oddly comforting when Marguerite was with him. He could lose himself within the nest of her warm, white arms more completely than had ever been possible to him before. Her dark eyes were like velvet with passion, and her little gasps of love, only half simulated, led him on and on into all the mazy, misty byways of sodden animalism. From Marguerite at least he had value for his money.

Even the awakening next morning, blear-eyed and foul-mouthed, was not as wretched as might have been thought. For at least he had grateful solitude, and to Mr

Marble solitude was very grateful, unless he had Marguerite with him. There was no wife with the anxious look in her eyes to worry him; he could roam round the house and satisfy himself for the thousandth time that the garden was undisturbed; he could dress himself slowly and leave the house without all the fuss of saying good-bye. He was usually half an hour late, of course, but that did not matter. He knew that dismissal from the office was near and inevitable, but he did not mind. Every day he could see in the eyes of the junior partner who had been so diffident about offering him five hundred a year a growing annoyance at his sodden appearance and unpunctual habits. Of course, he had done nothing to earn the salary he received. He had assisted the firm to no grand *coup* like the one he had brought off for himself. That—he had known it all along—was most unlikely now that he no longer had the spur of imminent necessity. But the new firm could dismiss him when it liked. He had twelve hundred a year of his own, and he did not want to be bothered with business. So to the office he went, red-eyed, unshaven, with shaking hands. His scanty red hair was fast turning grey.

The rest of the Marble family was endeavouring to enjoy itself. Some of its members were successful in varying degrees. The trio itself had been the object of amusement to the loungers in the palm-shaded entrance hall. Mrs Marble was so badly dressed, despite Winnie's misguided efforts, and she was so obviously frightened of porters and waiters; Winnie herself had roused some interest in a few breasts. She was young, anyone could see that, but not one of them guessed how young she was. Her clothes simply called for comment, and her actions likewise. Her face was over-powdered, and she was developing a habit of looking sidelong at the men in the lounge as she walked past them. That mixture of youth and innocence and yet apparent readiness awoke strange longings in the hearts of some of the old men who viewed her.

The cunning ones approached the mother first. There were chance conversations arising out of nothing in the hotel lounge, and Mrs Marble was agreeably surprised to have men with grey hair and the most perfect manners treating her with as much respect as if she were a duchess. She was flushed and flustered, but it was very nice to have the society of these gentlemen. One or two of them gave her the pleasure of dining at her table with herself and her daughter, and sometimes one would accompany them on some excursion to places in the neighbourhood. Winnie thoroughly enjoyed herself.

There were one or two young men, too, who scraped acquaintance with the queer party. One of them dropped out when he discovered that Mrs Marble did not possess much jewellery, and, in fact, did not care for jewellery, but the others stayed on. They danced with Winnie in the evenings, or took her 'just for the rag' to the local theatre. They were nearly annoyed when they found that Mrs Marble took it for granted that she was to accompany them; but there was no thought in her mind save just that. She could not picture a state of affairs in which anyone would sooner be alone with her daughter than have her present as well. But the men, young and old alike, found that there was one sure way of enjoying Winnie's society unadulterated; that was to settle Mrs Marble comfortably on the pier listening to the band, in a deckchair, and then take Winnie for a walk round. Mrs Marble was quite pleased when she found how attentive the men all were to her, and to what pains they went to see that she was quite comfortable and had all she wanted. It was a pleasant change from seventeen years odd of married life with William Marble. And it was astonishing how often Winnie replied to Mrs Marble's question: 'What would you like to do this morning?' (or this afternoon), with the ready response, 'Oh, let's go on to the pier and listen to the band, Mother.'

But amid all this enjoyment John was not enjoying himself. There was no place in the Grand Pavilion Hotel where he could sit and read in comfort, and the beach and the promenade were too crowded to permit such a thing either. He always had the Giant Twin, of course, but he did not always want to be out on it. Motor-cycling, even on the finest example of the finest make of motor-cycle in the world, begins to pall a little after three weeks' enforced indulgence, and there came a time when John was frankly bored. He was bored with hotel meals, with hotel friends, and with hotel public rooms. Music at his meals ceased to have any attraction for him at all. The men who sought Winnie's society looked upon him as an unmitigated nuisance, and were not too careful about concealing their opinion. And Winnie held the same opinion and did not try to conceal it at all. He could not even discuss motor-bicycles with anyone, in that he never met anyone who had ever owned such a thing.

John was bored, utterly and absolutely. After a fortnight's stay he hinted as much to his mother, but hints were not very effective in his mother's case. Three days later he tried again, with equal unsuccess. When he had endured three whole weeks he took the bit between his teeth and announced his intention of going home.

'But, my dear, why?' asked Mrs Marble.

John did his best to explain, but he felt from the start it was hopeless. The intuition proved correct, for Mrs Marble had no sympathy at all with boredom, never being bored herself.

'I don't think father will like it if you go home,' said Mrs Marble. 'He's spent an awful lot on this holiday for you, and you ought to show that you appreciate it.'

'But there's nothing to *do*,' expostulated John.

'Why, there's lots and lots to do, dear. You can listen to the band, or you can go out on the motor-bike, or—or —oh, there's lots to do. A great active boy like you ought to find things to do as easily as anything.'

'A great active boy can't listen to a band all day and all night,' said John, 'even if I was a boy, and even if I *liked* listening to bands, which I don't, very much. Hang it, I can't get hold of any decent books to read, and when I do I can't find anywhere to read them.'

'Don't argue with him, Mother,' cut in Winnie. 'He's only finding fault.'

'Finding fault' was in Mrs Marble's eyes a sort of vice to which the male sex was peculiarly prone at inconvenient moments. She suffered on account of it on occasions when Mr Marble's temper was not all that it should have been. Winnie seized the advantage conferred upon her by this dexterous tactical thrust.

'I don't see why he shouldn't go home, if you ask me,' she said. 'He'd be company for father, and it's only for a week, when all's said and done.'

Her arguments were not particular happy, for Mrs Marble remembered with a slight shudder the time when she had flung herself between her son and her husband. And she would be positively unhappy, whenever she remembered to be, at the thought of two helpless males alone in a house which cost her so much pains to run. But Winnie had her own reasons for wishing John away, reasons not unconnected with walks upon the pier and with visits to local cinematograph theatres.

'I should let him go,' said Winnie. 'Then he can collect a few of the mouldy old books he wants to read. He'll soon get fed up with being at home, and then he can come down here again. It'll only be for a day or two. He won't stand cooking his own breakfast longer than that. Then he'll be able to tell you how father's getting on.'

It was a wily move. Mrs Marble, in the intervals between being intimidated by waiters and chambermaids and enjoying the luxury they represented, was occasionally conscience-stricken about her deserted husband. She heard from him very little—only one or two straggling scrawls that told her nothing. More would have meant too much trouble to Mr Marble. Winnie's suggestion was therefore well timed.

'Well, do that then, dear,' said Mrs Marble. 'Go home just for the night and get all the books and things you want. Of course, if father doesn't mind, you can stay longer if you like. But you mustn't do anything that might make him cross.'

It was hardly the free-handed *congé* that Winnie would have liked her to give, but, still, it was something.

When John announced his intention of starting off at once Mrs Marble was shocked into protest. To her there was something unthinkable in changing one's place of abode at ten minutes' notice. She succeeded in persuading her son into postponing his departure until the next day—Saturday.

Even then she was full of instructions at the last moment.

'You know where the clean sheets are, don't you, dear?' she said. 'They're in the lowest drawer in the big chest of drawers. Mind you air them before you put them on your bed. Oh, and when you come down again will you bring my white fur? It's getting rather cold in the evenings now. You're sure you know the way home all right? It's rather a long way to go all by yourself.'

John had often before covered three times the distance in a single day, but he forbore saying so. He felt that it would be wiser to let his mother run on and have her full say out and then he would clear off without further argument. She continued, unmindful:

'I shall be quite anxious to hear that you got home safely. Mind you write as soon as you're there, and be sure you tell me how father is. And—and—don't forget what I said about not doing anything to annoy father.'

That made John fidget uneasily in his chair. At long last Mrs Marble ended with:

'Well, good-bye, dear. Have a good time. Have you got enough money? Then good-bye. Don't forget what I said. We're just going on the pier with Mr Horne. Good-bye, dear.'

And Winnie and Mrs Marble and Mr Horne were gone.

That was a most enjoyable day for John. For once he was neither the hotel prisoner nor yet was he at home with his father. It was the transition stage. He spent his time deliciously, luxuriously. He bathed by himself, at the far end of the town—his last bathe before starting out for home. That took time, for he wanted to make the most of it. Then he came back to the Grand Pavilion Hotel, took the Giant Twin from the garage, where it stood impatient and intolerant of all these domesticated saloons and limousines. The kick starter swung obediently, and the engine broke into its sweet thunderous roar. John swung himself into the saddle, and the Giant Twin sprang impatiently forward as he let in the clutch. They climbed the steep ascent of the side street without an effort, nosed their way through the squalor of the slums at the back of the town, and in fifteen minutes were out on the free open downs. But John was determined not to waste a minute of his day's happiness. He curbed the ardour of the Giant Twin to a mere fourteen miles an hour—a Rosinante speed worthy of his quixotic mood, as he told himself. They ambled along the great high road in wonderful spirits. The wind blew past him gently, and he filled his lungs with it, sighing with pleasure. It was twelve o'clock when he started; by one o'clock not thirty miles—not half the way—had been covered. John lunched by himself at a big yet homely hotel by the roadside. It was a decided change from lunch at the Grand Pavilion Hotel, with a band blaring only ten feet away, and mother talking platitudes—she couldn't help that, poor dear, but it grew wearisome after a week or two—and Winnie looking round discreetly at the men, or, worse, chattering away to some greasy-haired fellow she had wangled mother into inviting. They were all greasy-haired, somehow, and not one of them knew how to speak to a fellow, not even the young ones. And as for the old ones! There was one doddering old idiot who had asked him if he kept white mice! John stretched his legs in comforting fashion under the table and lit a cigarette. Thank God, that was over, anyway. He couldn't have borne that place another day. He hoped he would be all right with father. Father was such an uncertain sort of fellow nowadays. But apparently all he wanted was to be left alone, and that was all he wanted, as well. So they ought to get on all right. If they didn't—well, it couldn't be as bad as the hotel, anyway, with mother fussing over him and Winnie scrapping all the time. There was a little bit of the boor and a little bit of the bear about John.

But he was light-hearted enough when he came down and started up the Giant Twin once more for the last run homeward. He still went slowly, partly of his own free will, partly because of the growing volume of Saturday traffic that he met. He turned away from Croydon, and the Giant Twin brought him triumphantly up the long hill to the Crystal Palace without an effort. Ten minutes later the motor-bicycle ran silently with the clutch out, down the slope of Malcolm Road, and pulled up gently outside Number 53. John dismounted slowly.

It had been a glorious day. Even now it was not yet evening. There was nothing better than a late afternoon in August, at the end of a flaming day. The rather depressing little road looked positively heavenly to the exile after three weeks at the Grand Pavilion Hotel. There was just a touch of red in the sky, where the sun was beginning to sink. John was half smiling as he looked round him, while he fumbled in his pocket for his latch-key. He was even smiling as he put the key in the lock, and as he walked into the house.

Mr Marble had lately been looking forward to his Saturday afternoons. Following a lazy morning at the office, and a lazy lunch in town, he could travel quietly homeward after the rush. And at home, for in this case it was worth daring the watchfulness of the neighbours, especially considering that arriving as she did before he came back they might well think that she had come on some neighbourly errand in bringing shopping or to see that all was well in the house, there would be waiting for him Madame Collins, Marguerite—Rita, he called her nowadays. And they would have the whole afternoon and evening before them. She would not be leaving before dark. It would be a wonderful day. Eat, drink, and be merry, for to-morrow you die. Mr Marble ate, and most decidedly he drank, and he was merry as well, if such a term can be applied to his nightmare feeling of wild abandon. And the abandon was only possible because he was at 53 Malcolm Road, and able to make sure that there was no chance of his dying suddenly yet awhile.

John came into the dining-room. There was no one there. But the sight of the room brought the first chill to his heart. The gilded furniture blazed tawdrily in the fading sunlight; the room was in an indescribable muddle: dirty dishes and empty bottles were littered about it, and cigarette ash and cigarette ends were strewn over the floor. And in the room there was a subtle and distasteful blend of scents. Overlying the stale tobacco smell and the fustiness of unopened windows was the smell of spilt drink, and permeating the whole there was yet another odour, slight yet penetrating—a stale, unpleasant smell as of degraded hyacinths. John's nose wrinkled in distaste as the vile reek assailed his nostrils. The drink, and the tobacco, and the fustiness, and the muddle he could account for, and he had been prepared for them on a smaller scale. But this other scent, irritating his clean boy's palate, was different. It was more unclean even than the others.

He left the room hurriedly. He had already half decided that his father was not at present in the house. He set his foot on the stairs to go to his own room to open the windows, open them wide, so that the clean evening air would circulate there at any rate, but he withdrew it as a thought struck him. Most probably his father was in the back room—it had been his habit for a long time now to sit there on most occasions. If he were there, and if, as John reluctantly admitted to himself was most likely, he were drinking, it would be well for him to go in and report his arrival as soon as might be. His father would be furious if he were in the house without his knowledge. John walked back to the drawing-room, turned the handle of the door, and entered.

But he went no farther than just beyond the threshold. There he stopped, for a sickening, hellish two seconds, while the hyacinth scent rushed in greater volume upon him, its presence now explained, and while the sight that met his eyes struck him dazed, as might a club. It was sickening, bestial, abominable. He fled in a staggering run, fumbling in dazed haste at the handle of the door. To blend with the tumult of horrible remembrance came the sight, just as he reached free air again, of his father lurching after him, mumbling some wild words which he could not catch, but whose import clearly was for him not to go away, but to stay while he could explain. But John fled.

There was nothing else he could do. Every cell of his body called for air, air, air. Air to flood away that loathsome reek of hyacinths; air to flood his brain and blot away that memory of beastly, drunken nudity; air, air, air!

At the edge of the pavement stood his one trusty friend, the Giant Twin, who never would betray him. He leaned upon the friendly saddle for a second, while his whirling mind recovered itself to the slight degree possible. Air, air, air! He flung himself into the saddle, hands going automatically to ignition and throttle. The engine was still hot, and broke into its old friendly roar as he thrust at the kickstarter. Next second he was gone, wheeling wildly in the road, with the engine bellowing jubilantly as he forced the throttle wider.

The sunset was spreading over the sky, blood-red and tawny, as the sun vanished behind the houses, but it was still stiflingly hot. The air that raced past John's cheeks might as well have come straight from a blast-furnace. It raced past his cheeks, tugged at his hair, filled his lungs to bursting, and yet it gave no relief. Wider and wider went the throttle, and now the Giant Twin was hurtling along the roads as though they were a racetrack. John did not know where he was going, nor did he care. Air was what he wanted, air, more air. He sat well back in the saddle, while the tornado of his own begetting wrenched at him with a myriad fingers. Yet as he did so he shuddered at the recollection of the reek of hyacinth scent. The throttle was wide open now, and they were swirling round corners at an acute angle amid a shower of flying grit. Air, more air! John's hand moved to a forbidden lever, and the Giant Twin leaped forward even faster as the exhaust roared in thunder past the cutout.

It could not last. Not even the Giant Twin, ever loyal, could hold on those glassy roads at that speed. One last corner, and then the tyres lost their grip on the hardly noticeable camber. The Giant Twin leaped madly, plunging across the road, across the pavement. A cruel brick wall awaited them, in one rending crash of ruin.

CHAPTER XI

THERE was misery, misery undisguised and rampant, at 53 Malcolm Road. There were only two people living there now. Winnie had gone back to school, glad to escape from her mother's helpless unhappiness and her father's brooding gloom. But Mr Marble and Mrs Marble were there all the time. The blow of Mr Marble's dismissal from the new firm had fallen almost at once. He did not mind. He did not need the money, and it was such a terrible trouble to have to go up to the office every day. Unhappiness or no unhappiness, he preferred being at home, with his eye on the backyard and his pet books on crime and medical jurisprudence round him, to hanging about at the office all day, worrying about what was happening at home. And the sombre life of sitting solitary at home began to have a hideous fascination for him. There was no effort about it, no call for original thought or talent, and absence of effort was grateful to a man who habitually drank more than he should do, and whose mind was continually wandering down dark avenues, often traversed but always new. His wife was a nobody now, a phantom less real than the squint-eyed hangman that so often came tapping him on the shoulder; she was a soft-footed ghost that wandered about the house, coping ineffectually with the work that awaited her, and usually weeping, but so quietly that it did not disturb him. Sometimes Mrs Marble wept at the memory of her dead son; sometimes she wept because her back hurt her. But she wept at other times, too, and she did not know why she did; actually she was weeping because her husband had ceased to love her. Very grey, very frail and very, very unhappy was Mrs Marble at this time.

It was a strange, mad life that the two of them led nowadays. There was money in plenty, and very little use for it. The walls of the sitting-room were by now completely lined with Mr Marble's collection of books on crime; all the other rooms were crowded with massive and incredibly costly furniture, whose elaborate carvings were a source of woe to Mrs Marble when she came to dust them. The tradespeople had left off calling, nearly all of them, and all the shopping was done by Mrs Marble in hurried little excursions to the poverty-stricken shops near. There was money for servants, money for expensive and delightful foods, money for comfortable and manageable furniture. But no servant ever entered 53 Malcolm Road; the elaborate furniture was Mrs Marble's most weary burden, and for food they began to depend more and more upon ready cooked food bought as each meal came round in turn to augment the neglected store of the empty larder. Mrs Marble had begun to neglect her duty of housekeeping long ago. But she had only begun to show incapacity of this order since John's death.

In point of fact, Mrs Marble had an idea, and was

worrying over it. And when Mrs Marble wanted to work anything out by sheer force of brain-power she was compelled to abandon all her other labours in order to devote all her time to the task. She was working something out slowly, but, as is always the case when mentalities of that sort are once bent upon completing a task, very, very surely. Yet even now she could not have expressed her suspicions in words, so obscure were they. But they were not connected with Madame Collins, strange to relate.

Stranger still, it was this latter, dexterous though she was, who was the cause of the breakdown of the unstable state of affairs then prevailing. Those sums of money which she had received from Mr Marble had only whetted her appetite for more. They had made a wonderful difference to the bank balance over which she gloated in private. Yet that bank balance was not nearly large enough yet for her purpose, increased though it was by sums wrung from the allowance made by her husband for housekeeping. Madame Collins took it very ill that Mrs Marble should continue to stand in the way of her obtaining more.

For Mrs Marble did. No more would Mr Marble leave his house unguarded; no more could he be induced to relax his straining attention over that barren ten square yards of soil at the back of 53 Malcolm Road. For his obsession had grown upon him naturally as he gave it more play. In the days when it had been natural for him to go up to town every day it had been natural for his garden to take care of itself, but as soon as he had got into the comforting habit of watching over it continually he was unable to break himself of it. So he could not see her outside of his house, and in the house there was always his wife.

Madame Collins fretted and fumed. That bank balance of hers was mounting only by shillings a week when it ought to be mounting by pounds. She played desperately hard for fortune. She was as sweet as honey always to Mrs Marble. Yet it was not easy to gain Mrs Marble's good graces. Anxiety about her husband occupied such of her attention as was not busy working out the problem she had set herself. And she resented bitterly any display of sympathy, for that might indicate that the sympathizer understood her trouble better than she did herself. Besides, Mrs Marble had been 'respectably brought up', in a world where it was a serious social slur to have a drunken husband, and any reference to her husband's failing had her up in arms at once.

And Madame Collins had indiscreetly—though she herself had thought at the time that it was a good stroke of tactics—let it be known that she understood what was the matter with Mr Marble, to find to her surprise that Mrs Marble hotly resented her knowledge. To this cause for dissension must be added the fact that now that Mrs Marble had admitted to herself her failure to live the life of a rich woman, and her inability to wear good clothes as if she had always been accustomed to them, she had a bitter envy of those who were more successful. She disliked Madame Collins for her opulence of figure and good looks, for the way in which she wore her clothes, for the very clothes she wore. But Mrs Marble's dislikes were as unremarkable as everything else about her, and she was unable to show them except by a faint and rather bewildered hostility, which Madame Collins was able to sweep aside. It was more than Mrs Marble was capable of to be actively rude to anyone. So Madame Collins continued to call at rather frequent intervals, to talk in honey-sweet fashion to Mrs Marble, and sometimes to penetrate into that well-remembered sitting-room, if Mr Marble was not too fuddled, and to leave there a haunting scent of hyacinths and a clinging memory of rich flesh which sometimes penetrated into

Mr Marble's drink-sodden mind. Generally, however, it roused little fresh longing in him; he was at the moment amply content with his books and his drink and the knowledge that he was guarding that garden.

Mr Marble was rarely quite drunk. He never tried to be. All he ever attempted was to reach the happy stage —after the grim preliminary period when his imagination had been stimulated—when he was unable to think connectedly, so that he could not work out the long trains of thought that led inevitably to the picturing of detection and the scaffold. He could reach this stage comfortably quite early in the morning before the effects of the previous day's drinking had worn off, and then he was able to keep like it for the rest of the day by the simple mechanical process of drinking every time he found his thoughts taking an unpleasant line. The system was not the result of careful planning; it was merely the natural consequence of the situation, and for a long time it worked well enough. Comfortably hazy in his thoughts, comfortably seated in his armchair by the sitting-room window, with a new book on his knee to glance at occasionally—publishers' announcements were almost all the post delivered nowadays, and Mr Marble bought two books on crime a week on the average— Mr Marble almost enjoyed his life. His wife meant little to him, save that she was a convenient person to send out, green string bag in hand, to the grocer's to buy more whisky when his reserve dropped below the amount he had fixed upon—two untouched bottles. Mr Marble ate little; his wife ate even less; there was little enough work to keep Mrs Marble employed although she toiled inordinately hard in helpless fashion to keep the house in order. Mrs Marble spent her days wandering round the house soft-footed, slipshod, touching and fumbling and replacing. Her mind was busy trying to work something out.

It was through the agency of Madame Collins that she found the first clue to what she sought. Madame Collins had called in that evening as was her frequent habit and Mr Marble had been just a little more sober than usual. In consequence the evening meal had been spent in the sitting-room, and supper—a scratch meal, typical of Mrs Marble—had been served there. When the time came for Madame Collins to take her departure, Mr Marble, surprisingly enough, had risen slowly to his feet with the intention of seeing her home. Mrs Marble raised no objection; *that* was not what she was worrying about —yet. There had been a brief delay while Mr Marble was cramming his feet into his boots, soft feet, that for a week had known no greater restraint than that imposed by carpet slippers, and then they were gone. Mrs Marble remained in the sitting-room. Once alone, her old rest-lessness reasserted itself. She began to wander round the room, touching, fumbling, replacing. She was seeking something, nothing in particular, just something. Really it was the solution of her problem that she was seeking.

Round the room went Mrs Marble. She gazed for a space out of the window through which her husband stared so hard all day long, but it was quite dark outside and she could see nothing besides her own reflection. She picked up one or two of the ornaments on the mantel-piece, and put them back again. She ran her finger along the backs of the books that stood on the shelves. They did not interest her. Then she came to the book that lay on the arm of her husband's chair, the book he had been reading in desultory fashion during the day. Mrs Marble picked it up and ran the pages through her fingers. It was not an interesting book. She did not even know what the title—somebody or other's *Handbook of Medical Jurisprudence*—meant. But at one point the book fell open of its own accord, and the open pages were well thumbed, proving that this portion had received more attention than the rest of the book. It was in the section on Poisons, and the paragraph was headed 'Cyanides—Potassium Cyanide, Sodium Cyanide'. A tiny wrinkle appeared between Mrs Marble's brows as she read this. She cast her mind back to that morning many months ago now, the morning after Medland's dramatic arrival. Yes, that was the name on the label of the bottle she had found displayed on Will's shelves. Potassium Cyanide. She went on to read what the book had to say on the subject.

'Death is practically instantaneous. The patient utters a loud cry and falls heavily. There may be some foam at the lips, and after death the body often retains the appearance of life, the cheeks being red and the expression unaltered.'

The wrinkle between Annie Marble's brows was deeper now, and her breath was coming faster. She could remember what she had heard when she was half asleep the night of Medland's coming. She had heard Will come up to the bathroom where his chemicals were kept, and she had heard him go down again. Then she had heard that loud cry.

In her next deduction her memory was at fault, but it was a fault that, curiously enough, confirmed her suspicions. Annie thought she remembered hearing a heavy fall at the same time as that loud cry. Of course she had not done so; young Medland had been sitting in a chair at the time when Marble said 'Drink up', but Annie was not to know that. Influenced by what she had read, Annie was quite certain that she had heard that heavy fall. Now she knew what it was she had heard dragged through the passage down the stairs to the kitchen. And she guessed whither it had been taken from the kitchen. She knew why Will spent all his time watching through the window to see that the garden was not interfered with. The problem with which she had been wrestling for weeks was solved. She felt suddenly weak, and she sank into the chair. All her other memories, crowding up now unsummoned, confirmed her solution. She could remember how there was suddenly more money at their disposal, and how Will had comported himself the next morning. She was sure of it all.

As she lay back in the chair, weak and wretched, she was startled to hear her husband's key in the door. She made a spasmodic effort to hide what she was doing, but she was too weak to achieve anything. Her husband entered the sitting-room while she still held the book open in her hand. Her thumb was between the pages, at the point where there was that interesting description of the effects of potassium cyanide.

When Mr Marble crossed the threshold, he uttered an angry exclamation as he saw what Mrs Marble was doing. He would tolerate no interference with his precious library. He strode forward to snatch the book out of her hand. Mrs Marble sat helpless, and made no resistance. She even held out the book a little to him, offering it to his grip. But as she did so the book fell open at the place where she held it, fell open at the passage on the cyanides.

Mr Marble saw this. He saw the look on her face, too. He stopped aghast. There was no need for words. In that brief space of time he realized that his wife knew. That she *knew*.

Neither of them said anything; neither of them was capable of saying anything in that tense moment. They eyed each other in poses curiously alike, she with her hand to her bosom as she peered at him, fluttering, tearful, and he with his hand, too, over his heart. Just lately he had not noticed so much the inconvenient tendency of that organ to beat with such violence, but now it was impressed upon him again. It thundered in his breast, depriving him of his strength, so that he had to hold on to a chair-back to support himself.

Annie gave a little, inarticulate cry. The book fell to the ground from her hand, and then sobbing, she fled from the room without again meeting his eye.

CHAPTER XII

THERE is no solitude like that which one can find in a London suburb. It is desolate, appalling. The weeks that passed now found the Marbles lost in this solitude, and over them, like a constant menace, hung the unvoiced menace of a secret shared. The days they spent together in the tawdry rooms downstairs; the nights they spent together in the vast gilt bed in the front bedroom, but for all that they were each of them lonely and frightened. The weight of their secret prevented all conversation save that about the necessary commonplaces of house-keeping, and even this they restricted self-consciously to the uttermost minimum. They did not exchange a dozen words a day; they said nothing, did nothing; they thought about nothing save the one dreadful thing about which they dared not speak. The solitude of the suburbs which they experienced was theirs from choice; they had cut themselves off voluntarily from their neighbours, and the neighbours in turn withdrew from them, sneering to each other about Mrs Marble's unhappy new clothes and the gorgeous furniture that they could see through the lower windows at Number 53. But this isolation was hardly new and was easily borne; it was far otherwise with the spiritual separation that encompassed them each individually.

They were living together alone in the tiny house; they were in each other's society from choice—they each soon found that they could not bear to have the other for long out of their sight—but not once in weeks did their eyes meet. And never, never did they make any comment on their isolation.

Back into this nightmare world came Winnie, flushed with triumphs at school. She was undoubtedly beautiful now, and she was dressed to perfection, as soon as she had thrown off the shackles imposed by school rules. Her beauty had won over to her one party at school, and her almost unlimited pocket-money had won over another. Eleven months only younger than her dead brother, she was now just sixteen; a thoroughly good preliminary education at the secondary school—to which she looked back with horror, and about which she had always been discreetly silent—had saved her much trouble as regards actual school work and had placed her in the highest form after one term there. Miss Winifred Marble had the very highest opinion of herself.

She came home in typical fashion. She had given her parents no exact information of the time of her return, and she was more or less unexpected when her taxicab drew up outside Number 53 Malcolm Road. She descended leisurely to the pavement. Malcolm Road might indeed be to her mind a horrible hole, but for all that she was not going to miss one tenth of the sensation she was aware she was making therein. She could see hurried heads appearing behind the curtains at all the houses around, and she allowed the neighbours ample time to view her mountainous luggage piled on the roof of the cab, and to admire enviously her smart blue costume. With a brief order to the driver to bring in her luggage she marched up the front path and knocked at the door with a resounding rat-tat-tat.

Indoors her father and mother were sitting together in the back room, he with a book on his knee as usual, she gazing into vacancy, following in her vague fashion all the unpleasant lines of thought that her husband had followed long ago. At the sound of Winnie's knocks Marble rolled a frightened eye upon her. She rose in heart-fluttering panic.

'Will,' she said, 'it's not—it's not—?'

Only police would knock like that at 53 Malcolm Road. Marble could make no answer for the moment. The knocking came again. Marble tried with shaking hands to light himself a cigarette. Come what may, he must try to look nonchalant, to bear himself calmly, as did all those men he had read about in his books when the fatal moment of arrest arrived. But his hands shook too much. His very lips were trembling, so that the cigarette quivered like a reed between them. The knocking was repeated. Then at last Mrs Marble rallied.

'I'll go,' she said, in a weak whisper.

Down the passage she went, soft-footed, ghostlike. Marble, still fumbling with his cigarette, heard the door open, after what seemed like ages of waiting. Then he heard Mrs Marble say: 'Oh, my dear, it's you. Oh, dearie ——' and Winnie's lady-like voice answering her. With the relief from tension the matches dropped from his fingers. The cigarette sagged from his mouth. He leant sideways against the arm of his chair, his eyes staring, too weak to move, while his heart thudded and fluttered back to its usual rhythm. That was how they found him, Winnie and her mother, when they came into the sitting-room to his expected welcome.

Such was the household to which Winnie returned, three days before Christmas. The girls at school, who envied Winnie her trunkfuls of clothes and her ample pocket-money, had been talking for weeks about what they intended to do this holiday. There had been talk of hunting, of dances, of theatres. There had been comparisons between the food they had at school and the food they would have at home during this period of delectable food. And in all this conversation Winnie had borne a part by no means equal to the part she usually bore in school conversations. Yet she had called up all the help of her imagination, and with its aid she had been able to produce some sort of picture of similar enjoyment in prospect for herself. That made the disappointment all the more bitter. The Marble family lunched that day, the first day of her arrival, on cold ham and stale bread and butter, and not enough of either. Her father's clothes were baggy and spotted, and on his feet were wrecks of carpet slippers. He drank heavily of whisky during the meal, and he had obviously been drinking too much all the time she had been away. Her mother wore a shabby blouse and skirt, gaping wherever they could gape, and her stockings were in wrinkles up her thin calves. Winnie's eyebrows puckered, and her lips curled a little as she observed these things.

Then Mrs Marble noticed that Winnie was dissatisfied, and inevitably she bridled. She knew her housekeeping was at fault, but she was not going to have her sixteen-year-old daughter running down *her* house.

'Isn't there anything else to eat?' asked Winnie, when the last of the cold ham had disappeared, leaving her hungrier than when she started, accustomed as she was to the well-cooked and ample meals of the Berkshire school.

'No, there's not,' snapped Mrs Marble.

'But hang it all——' protested Winnie.

It was hardly the best of starts for a Christmas holiday. Winnie bore it for two days, and then, on Christmas eve, she began active operations. Her mother, whom she approached first, gave her no satisfaction.

'Oh, don't worry me,' she said, with a heat unusual for her, 'we've got enough to worry us as it is.'

'But what *have* you got to worry you?' said Winnie, genuinely bewildered. 'Worry or no worry, we've got enough money and all that sort of thing, haven't we?'

Mrs Marble clutched at this straw for a moment, but she was not adept at deception, and her faint-hearted statement that all was not well with them financially died away when she met Winnie's incredulous gaze.

'Don't be silly, mother,' said Winnie, and Mrs Marble meekly bowed her head to the storm.

'No, it's not money, dear. I'm sure your father gives me all I want in that way.'

'How much a week?' demanded Winnie, relentlessly.

Mrs Marble made a last desperate stand against this implacable woman who had developed so surprisingly out of the little daughter she had once been.

'Never you mind,' she said. 'It's *my* business, and this is *my* house, and you've no right to interfere.'

Winnie sniffed.

'No right,' she said, 'when you've given me cold ham three times and pressed beef once in two days? Do you know to-morrow's Christmas, and I don't believe you've done anything yet towards it? And look at your clothes! It's worse than the last time I came home. I'm sure that before I went back to school I left you all nicely rigged out. You had such a nice costumes, and—and——' This was a false step, for neither Winnie nor her mother was yet able to bear a reference to poor dead John, for whom Mrs Marble had bought mourning with Winnie's help last holiday.

'Be quiet, do,' said Mrs Marble, with tears in her eyes.

They were not entirely tears of mourning, but they quelled Winnie effectively. Even she felt a little shy and embarrassed at sight of her mother crying. So she relaxed her inquiry, just when a little more pressing would have forced from her mother the astonishing facts that Mr Marble was prepared for her to spend ten pounds a week on her housekeeping while she actually only spent two —hardly as much as she had spent before they attained to riches.

But Winnie was at least persistent. After her mother she approached her father, daring even to break in upon his whisky-sodden reverie in the drawing-room.

'Father,' said Winnie, 'are we dreadfully poor since you left off going to the City?'

Mr Marble rolled a maudlin eye upon her. Then pride reasserted itself—pride in his achievement all those months ago, which was still mentioned with bated breath by City clerks, but which had never received its meed of recognition in his own home.

'No,' he said. 'We've got plenty.'

'That's good. It's Christmas to-morrow. I want some money. Lots of it. Mother hasn't done anything about it yet.'

Far back in Mr Marble's dulled memory ghosts began to stir. He remembered those times—they seemed ages ago now—when he wanted his wife to spend money, and had had all the difficulty in the world to induce her to do so.

He rolled obediently out of his chair and walked almost steadily across to the ridiculous gilt bureau in the corner of the room. He fumbled it open; fumbled out his cheque-book; fumblingly signed a cheque.

'Banks shut at half-past three,' he said. 'Better be quick.'

Winnie only had to give a fleeting glance at the cheque. It was for one hundred pounds.

'Thank you,' she said, and before she had left the room she was calling to her mother to put her hat on.

Mrs Marble had never been so hurried and flurried in her life before as she was that Christmas eve.

There was the rush to get the bus to Rye Lane. Then there was the rush to the bank to cash the cheque. Winnie put the money in her handbag as if she was accustomed to having a hundred pounds there every day of her life. Then there was a series of rushes up and down Rye Lane, crowded with Christmas shoppers, buying everything which Mrs Marble had omitted to buy, which comprised a good many necessities as well as the inevitable luxuries of Christmas. She was almost dropping with unaccustomed fatigue when Winnie hailed a heaven-sent taxicab that appeared and piled her and the myriad parcels they had accumulated into it.

Yet even this did not satisfy Winnie. She was not even satisfied with bullying her mother next day into cooking turkey and reheating the ready-made Christmas puddings they had bought. She was not satisfied with insisting on having a clean cloth on the table and all the silver displayed thereon. She was not satisfied with giving presents —bought with the money obtained yesterday—to her father and mother, and with showing them what they had bought for her from the same source. She was not satisfied with hanging holly and mistletoe all over the house. Even when Christmas Day was over and her parents thought they had suffered all they could, she began to go systematically through the house 'putting things straight'. That Berkshire school prided itself on the domestic training it gave its girls—domestic training on a scale calculated for women who would not be likely ever to have dealings with the economics of a house of thirty pounds a year rateable value into which no servant or even charwoman was allowed ever to set foot. Winnie's ideas were on the grand scale.

She succeeded in upsetting Mrs Marble, and by natural reaction she upset her father as well. Mr Marble had been unhappy before, but it was a negative and inactive unhappiness. He had settled down into a groove, and a groove, with all its suggestion of permanency, was grateful to a man in the shadow of the gallows. Any disturbance of that groove was annoying. He had grown used to being badly fed, and he never noticed the other details of household management. He had even ceased long since from having any pride in his Empire furniture. But Winnie with her bustle and hustle disturbed him. Without realizing it, he had taken comfort from his wife's inaction, knowing that that meant there was less chance of her giving away the secret he knew she held in her bosom. And now Winnie had descended upon them to alter all this. He did not like it. He liked it still less when he found that Winnie had her eye upon his drinking habits and was meditating interfering with them as well.

But happily Winnie was not of the stuff that carries things through to the bitter end in face of all opposition. She was like her father in that she was able to make one big effort which achieved much but left her incapable of more for a considerable time. Her activity died down, and in a brief time she found herself actually acquiescing in some of Mrs Marble's shiftless methods of housekeeping. And in a flash she found that she was incredibly bored.

She had once more got her mother's wardrobe into some sort of order, and she had bullied and cajoled her into wearing the good clothes that were heaped untidily about her bedroom. By the time she had made her mother smart again, and had rearranged everything in accordance with the system that even only two terms at the school had ingrained into her, Winnie found that her interest in housekeeping was waning, and that life at 53 Malcolm Road was decidedly dull.

So she wrote off one or two letters, to friends of hers at school. It hardly matters what she put into them, whether it was fact or fiction, whether she wrote about illness—of course not infectious—at home, or about domestic unhappiness. Whatever it was she wrote, it achieved its object. She received very shortly afterwards two invitations to spend the rest of her holidays with these friends of hers.

By that time neither Mr nor Mrs Marble was sorry to see her go. She had caused too much disturbance altogether. So they said good-bye to her in a philosophic manner. Mr Marble, partly as a sheer thanksgiving offering, partly because Winnie took it as a matter of course, and partly even with a flicker of his old pride that a daughter of his should be going to stay as a guest at a house whose sole address was a name and a county, handed over another cheque. Life had grown so strange and unreal to them that they saw nothing out of the ordinary in letting a sixteen-year-old girl go away to stay with people they did not know, with something nearly approaching a hundred pounds in her handbag.

After all, Mr Marble's income was nearly twelve hundred a year; of that Winnie's fees amounted to nearly three hundred, but of the remaining nine he hardly spent a quarter. A man who has five hundred a year for which he can find no use does not worry about odd hundreds, especially when he spends every waking minute in terror of being hanged.

CHAPTER XIII

THE peace that had been so rudely disturbed was only with difficulty regained. The Marbles found it hard to settle down once more into the old groove. And no sooner had they begun to do so than another interruption to their peace—if their panic-stricken existence can be so called—occurred, this time at the hands of a more dangerous person, Madame Collins.

She had come to the limit of her patience. Nearly six months had elapsed since she had paid into her account a little roll of bank-notes which might have been traced, had anyone taken the trouble, to Mr Marble. After that last terrible occurrence, when that silly boy John had met with the motor-cycling accident, she had indeed been content to wait a while, until matters should be quieter again, but this wait was too long altogether. Dressmaking in a back street in Dulwich with an automaton of a husband began to annoy her exceedingly. Anything was better than that, she decided. Even at Christmas time she had meditated action, but Winnie had been there when she called, and Winnie had looked her up and down with cool insolence and even Marguerite Collins had been abashed—or, rather, had decided that it would be better if Winnie were not her enemy. She bided her time awaiting a more favourable moment.

One morning Mr Marble was alone at home, for Annie had gone out on one of her all too infrequent shopping expeditions. She had been gone five minutes only, when to Marble's ear came the familiar sound of her hurried, quiet knock. With an enormous effort—everything was a great deal of trouble nowadays—he heaved himself out of his chair and went to the door.

Marguerite Collins was determined to have no nonsense. As the door opened she stepped inside, and she was through into the drawing-room and sitting down before Marble had shut it again. Marble came and stood before her wearily and dull-wittedly. There was clearly going to be trouble, and Mr Marble did not feel in the mood for trouble.

'Well, what is it?' asked Marble.

Marguerite did not answer at once. She threw back the fur from round her neck and drew off her gloves with slow, deliberate movements. With a gesture she made much of her round, white throat and her plump hands. Six months ago this alone would have stirred Marble into action, but now it left him unmoved. Those six months had been spent in sluggish over-drinking and in frothy anxiety. Besides, he had had his will of her, and Marguerite was not of the type to revive dead passion. All this Marguerite realized as she watched, keenly but covertly, his unshaved face and the expressionless blue eyes. It was as she feared. Well, it would have to be pure business, then, without the frail disguise of anything else.

'You are not pleased that I come to see you?' she asked, with the lisp and trace of accent that Marble had once thought so wonderful.

'No,' said Marble, in no mood for tact. As a matter of fact, he was rapidly growing incapable of thinking about anything save what lay outside under the soil of the dreary backyard.

But the monosyllable roused Madame Collins to fury. It hurt, the more so as she had realized it previously.

'You are not polite,' she said, a faint flush appearing on her soft—over-soft—cheeks.

'No,' said Marble.

'You admit it! Are you not ashamed? And do you not remember when you would not have said a thing like that to me—no, not for worlds?'

'No,' said Marble.

'No, no, no! Have you nothing else to say to me except "no"?'

'No,' said Marble. He could hardly be said to be intentionally rude; but a man whose mind chooses that particular moment to run off on its favourite track towards arrest and execution is in no fit state to argue any point whatever with a hot-tempered woman—especially when he is in the wrong.

Marguerite Collins bit her lips, and then restrained herself by a violent effort of will. After all, money—so said her peasant soul to herself—was sweeter than revenge at any time, sweet though they both were; if she could obtain no money, then perhaps she could have the other, but she would spare no effort to screw more money out of this weak-minded *rentier* first.

She spoke calmly, and she allowed just as much of the old sweetness to creep into her tone as she thought might soften Marble towards her.

'Listen, Will. I am in trouble. I am in great trouble. My husband—you know what he is, I have told you, oh, so often—he is unsupportable. I hate him. And now I think—he hates me also. I must leave him. I must go away. I shall go back to Normandy, to Rouen. But I must have money. He has none. No more have I. Will, dear——'

Marble made one of the greatest mistakes of his life when he said 'no' for the fifth time that morning. The flush on Marguerite's cheeks became deeper; she was scarlet with indignation. It is doubtful why Marble should have said it; a single one of those unspent hundreds from his annual income would have ended the matter for the time. But the refusal slipped out of his mouth before he was aware of it; he was only trying to temporize. City caution told him that this was blackmail, and that it is fatal to yield to a blackmailer; he also realized at the back of his mind that he most certainly had not in the house at that moment enough ready money to satisfy her, and he was not going to give her a cheque—not he. So he said 'no' really meaning 'yes', and had he not been so dull-witted that morning he would have bitten his tongue out rather than have said it.

Marguerite condescended to use a threat or two.

'That is a pity,' she said, 'for I must have my freedom. If I were to tell my husband one or two little things—ah, he would set me free, do you not think so? But it would cost you much money, more than what I have stooped to ask you. And your wife, she would not like that to happen, would she? She does not know at present, eh? If you would like her to——?'

Marble's face had turned from pale to flushed and back again to pallor.

The stab had gone home. Anything rather than let Annie know. Annie held the key of his life in her hand; she had guessed his secret, he was sure of it. The knowledge had troubled him little up to the moment. She had been a cipher in his life for so long that he had hardly cared, save that it had made it uncomfortable to meet her eyes. But if Annie were to know of this! His drink-dazed mind realized for the first time how desperately necessary it was that Annie should be kept in a good humour. The terror in his breast made him lose control over himself.

'All right, I'll pay you,' he said. 'How much is it?'

He had cut the ground from under his feet. He had shown her which was the best course of action; he had shown her how much he feared Annie's knowing; by his earlier refusal and later hurried agreement he had delivered himself over bound and naked to his enemy. Marguerite laughed a little, a malicious, throaty laugh. Then she spoke, mentioning the sum quite as if it were a matter of course.

'Three hundred pounds.'

'I—I can't afford all that!'

The surprise in Mr Marble's voice was obvious and genuine; but Marguerite was quick-witted enough to see that he really could afford the huge sum.

'Three hundred pounds,' she said again.

'But I haven't got all that in the house, and a cheque ——'

'It is a cheque that I want,' said Madame Collins grimly, and seeing him still hesitate for a moment she added, 'And your wife will be back soon, will she not?'

Marble went over to the gilt bureau and wrote out the cheque.

She was just re-clasping her handbag when they heard Annie Marble's key in the door. When she entered the room Marble was the one that was obviously discomposed. She herself was honey-sweet as usual, calm and self-possessed.

'I have come to say good-bye,' she said. 'To-morrow I go to France.'

'To France?'

'Yes, I am going to have a holiday. I am sorry that you were out when I came for I have so much to do that I fear I cannot stay. No, no, really I cannot. Good-bye, dear Mrs Marble. I will send you a postcard from Rouen.'

With that she was gone. It was rather a pity that Mr Marble should have been so obviously anxious to get rid of her. Why, she herself was most anxious to be out of the house too, so that she could hurry and cash that cheque before Marble could stop it, if by chance he recovered his spirits enough to do anything like that, but she showed no signs of it at all. It was perfectly true that at the time Mrs Marble did not notice her husband's nervousness, but little things like that, as time had already shown, had a way of staying in Mrs Marble's memory and re-emerging at inconvenient moments.

After Madame Collins' departure Mr Marble eyed his wife anxiously. He had realized now that she was a person of immense importance to his affairs, and, what was more, that she was, after all, someone who might, should it so happen, act independently. He had grown so used all his life to regarding her as the very reverse of a free agent, as obedient to himself almost as one of his own limbs, that the reflection that she might not be so startled him. There was only one thing, Marble knew, that would make her break out contrary to his wishes, but that was the least accountable of all factors. If Annie got to know that he had been unfaithful to her; if she had it forced home upon her that his love for her—if ever it had existed; and it had in her imagination, which was all that mattered—was dead, then she would be capable of doing the most unexpected things. She would not deliberately betray him—not even terror-maddened Marble thought that—but she might in her consternation allow something to escape her that would set in action that swarm of rumours and the resultant investigation that Mr Marble so dreaded. It was of the first importance that she should continue to think he loved her. And the fact that he endowed this circumstance with its full importance was directly due to Madame Collins. At the moment he felt almost grateful to the latter for showing him this. But he eyed his wife anxiously, for all that. It was an added complication, and the burden of his troubles was already almost more than he could bear.

And yet perhaps, although Mr Marble did not appreciate it, this new complication was for the time at least a blessing in disguise. It took Mr Marble's mind off the main point of his troubles, and that was more than anything else had done during the last year. The situation reacted upon him in such a way that for twenty-four hours Mr Marble hardly drank any whisky at all.

But it was one thing to decide to make oneself agreeable to one's wife, and quite another to carry it out. Mr Marble felt positively embarrassed as he eyed his wife and tried to brace himself for action. He had lived with her in the closest proximity and yet in the harshest isolation for a year now; it would be a difficult matter to break the ice and start afresh. Besides, there lay between them the shadow of a terrible secret. That might serve to bind them closer together later on, but at present it was an obstacle almost insurmountable. Not all that day, not that night, not the next day did Mr Marble make much progress.

He made no progress in his own estimation, that is to say. Thirty-six hours after deciding upon this course of action Mr Marble still felt almost shy and almost embarrassed in his wife's presence. But Mrs Marble had noticed something. First and foremost, of course, she noticed that he was not drunk. That was obvious. This temperance was partly deliberate and partly reflex, dependent on Mr Marble's knowledge that it would be as well to keep his head clear, and to appear as attractive in his wife's eyes as possible. But partly it was due to the fact that, with this new problem to think about, Mr Marble had no thought to spare for his other troubles, and, consequently, no need to dull his mind to them.

But Mrs Marble noticed more than his soberness. She caught him repeatedly looking at her with an anxious air—the same manner as a courting lover might display. And he made one or two tentative attempts at conversation with her too. Seeing that he had said nothing to her for months save the one or two words that had to be said this was an enormous difference. He looked at her, he spoke to her, with a shyness that set her fluttering, and more than once he opened his mouth as though to say something to her and then held back at the last minute, obviously embarrassed. Mrs Marble felt strangely pleased. After all, dear Will was her whole life, especially now that John was no longer with her, and, secret or no secret, this new wooing in this strange shy fashion was grateful to her and gave her a warm, comforted, feeling.

It was the evening after Madame Collins' visit that it really began over again. They were sitting together in the back room, trying to talk, when Collins himself called.

Mrs Marble brought him in. He was a frail, pale, fair man, and he looked white and fagged. He sat down on the chair offered him with a sigh.

'I've come to see if you know anything about my wife,' he said wearily.

'What, Marguerite? Why, yes, she was here yesterday. She said she was just off for a holiday. Where was it she said she was going to, Will?'

'Normandy, of course,' said Marble. He wanted to appear to know as little as possible about the business.

'I thought as much,' sighed Collins.

Neither of the Marbles spoke, and after a moment Collins went on:

'She's gone. I suppose she's gone for good. I—I don't know whether she's gone alone though.'

'But didn't she say where she was going?' Mrs Marble was quite irrepressible this evening, as a result of her husband's flattering attentions.

'No. I didn't know that she was going. She took good care of that. She has taken everything with her.'

'Everything?' Mrs Marble did not understand.

'Everything. All our savings she's taken. All her own things, too. There's even a bill of sale on the furniture, I found this morning.' Collins was resting his forehead on his hands. 'She went yesterday,' he added inconsequently.

The Marbles felt the uselessness of trying to console him. No word was said for a space. Then Collins stood up and reached for his hat. He hesitated for a second.

'I'm sorry to have troubled you,' he said, weakly. 'But I—I just wanted to know.' Then, in a little spurt of feeling, he added, 'It's hateful to have to ask other people about my own wife. But—I didn't want her to go. I didn't want her to go.'

He almost broke down, but turned away and began to stumble to the door. Marble followed him. Halfheartedly, but in a man-of-the-world tone, he offered his help.

'If there's anything I can do, Collins——'

'I don't think there is,' said Collins, feebly.

'Money?'

'No, I won't want money. It was she who wanted money.'

Collins was feeling his way blindly, weakly, down the passage. His shoulders drooped. Clearly he was quite broken down by the desertion of his wife—much more than Marble had expected. It became obvious that Marguerite's tales of their unhappiness together had been one-sided.

'Well, if there *is* anything I can do——' said Marble again.

It was the inevitable feeble proffer of help, and Collins declined it once more. Then he went out into the night, with dragging feet, hardly able to walk. There were tears in Mrs Marble's eyes when Marble came back to her in the sitting-room.

'Poor man,' said she.

Marble nodded.

'And what a hateful woman she must be!' she went on. 'I thought the first time I saw her that she was—well, you know, like that.'

Mrs Marble had not thought anything of the kind; but she thought she did, after the event.

'Poor old Collins seems broken up about it,' was Marble's comment.

'He must have loved her a lot. Poor chap! And she's gone now, and left him alone. Hateful woman!'

The tears were even more imminent in her eyes now, as she stood by him, and there was a strange surge of emotion in her breast. Marble looked at her queerly. Both their hearts were throbbing tumultuously.

'You wouldn't do a thing like that, would you?' said Marble, his hands playing with her sleeves.

Annie looked up at his face for a second—only a second.

'Oh, how could I? Oh, Will, Will, dear.'

There was no more need for words. But as Marble kissed her—her cheeks were wet, too, by now—he felt a queer, guilty sensation internally. And yet he meant that kiss, he really did. Perhaps Judas felt the same once.

CHAPTER XIV

AND SO, incredible as it might seem, sunshine had come again for a space to 53 Malcolm Road. The black pall of terror was lifted, and Annie Marble actually went singing in her high, cracked voice up and down the stairs as she did her housework. Not one word had passed between them concerning the shade of terrible danger that brooded over them, but now that each knew, and had shown that they could bear with the knowledge, the shade did not seem so black. It was a trouble shared, and a trouble shared *voluntarily* is a trouble robbed of half its weight.

Singing, Annie Marble went up and down the stairs. Marble, sitting downstairs, could hear her thin voice and her light step. For the present the voice did not call up a scowl to his brow; nor did the step seem too stealthy to be tolerated, as once it did. Whisky had lost its savour for the time being; there was no pressing need for it to dull his mind. Most of the time Marble's mouth was twisted with a queer smile—and he had not smiled for months—as he thought of the difference his taking notice of his wife had made. He was glad of it, too, and now he could not think of his wife without that smile. He felt glad and comforted as he thought of her. Her present high spirits might be pathetic; they might even seem a trifle ridiculous, but they were, nevertheless, infectious. Within Mr Marble's bosom there was a fondness, almost a fatherly fondness, springing up for the woman who loved him so well.

And, estimating gains from the most sordid point of view it was a distinct advantage that he should have in the house a willing ally upon whom he could rely and who was possessed of sufficient knowledge of the facts of the case to help him should emergency arise.

Mr Marble was even able occasionally to throw off his obsession completely and leave the house—and the garden—to his wife's care, while he went forth through the dingy streets for exercise. The straggling rays of spring sunshine seemed to warm him, at a time when other people were hurrying along clasping their heavy coats to themselves in the bitter cold, and he blinked at the sunlight gratefully with house-blinded eyes.

As for Annie Marble, she was a changed woman. She could sing about the house; the housework seemed nothing to her nowadays, so comforting was the knowledge that darling Will was downstairs thinking about her; she routed out from some neglected kitchen shelf a stained copy of Mrs Beeton—a wedding gift, unlooked at since she first had two children on her hands, sixteen years ago—and laboured joyously, though rarely successfully, compounding new delicacies for her beloved lord. For now there was no pinch for money, and Annie had found sixteen years ago that if one wanted to cook in the style of Mrs Beeton there was a great need of money.

And the will had to be there, too. So the evenings often found her sitting laboriously composing notes to the big stores ordering all sorts of strange things, things which she had never thought of ordering before, bottled oysters, asparagus, *foie gras*, queer lists for which Mr Marble signed the cheques without a murmur. He felt that at last he was beginning to have some benefit from the money he had won at such risk during his slavery at the Bank. It was the first time.

And Mrs Marble's personal expenses, too, began to show a healthy increase. She did not venture up to Bond Street again, that was asking too much of her; she could not face the immense superiority of the young ladies in those shops; even High Street, Kensington, was a little above her head, but in Rye Lane she was exceedingly happy. The shops therein arrogantly called it 'the Regent Street of South London' in their advertisements, and they did their level best to live up to the boast. Mrs Marble's frail little figure and her witless face, made almost pretty by reason of her happiness, became well known there. She would flit around the big shops, ordering here, trying on there, with in her manner a little trace of apology for troubling the assistants, for all her money. For her it was one of the very keenest of enjoyments, so keen that it almost hurt, to buy things, anything she liked, without having to think about the cost. But always she would stop in the middle of her shopping and hurry anxiously to catch a bus to get home in case her darling Will was growing anxious about her.

Yet this happiness, this moment of peace, was only a lull in the storm. They were both conscious of this, although they never admitted it even to themselves. And because they would not admit it they were still handicapped in their relations with each other. Annie found this one morning when she came home from Rye Lane and found Marble sitting spiritlessly in his chair in the sitting-room, in almost the same way as he had sat in the dark days gone by. There was a cloud on his brow; she could tell that at once. But she tried to act naturally. She came fluttering up to him with all her parcels, dropped the latter carelessly on the table, and bent over and kissed him lightly, spontaneously—a trick she had never mastered before, not even in the honeymoon days.

'I've got back, you see,' said she. It was just the sort of thing one would expect her to say, and because of this it ought to have called up an instant smile; it would have done so yesterday.

But to-day there was no smile. Marble's set, dull look frightened her, it was so like the look he had worn in the bad time. A little shudder ran through her, as she realized that it was calling up within her the same sensations, as though they were echoes, that she had known during the same period. A light had gone out in the world.

'What's the matter, dear?' she said. 'Aren't you—aren't you well?' that was all she could say, because of the barrier still between them. She could not very well say: 'Is your conscience troubling you?' or 'Are you still afraid of detection?'

And Marble could only answer dully, 'Oh, I'm all right,' and put her aside rather abashed and frightened. He could not tell her that what he had foreseen had happened; that by the second post, happily after she had gone out, there had arrived a letter from Rouen, a cruel, bitter letter, delicately phrased and worded, apparently telling him of the writer's unbounded affection for him, but really only a sneering demand for money—more money. The actual cash did not matter so much; Marble had enough and to spare to keep even Marguerite Collins quiet. No, it was not the money. It was—although he did not allow himself to believe it—the fact that the letter had brought back into his life what had been for a moment absent—the sense of hideous insecurity, the knowledge that the future was laden with all sorts of ghastly possibilities, and had once more set his mind running on the things that might happen. Marble started drinking heavily again that day. He could hardly be blamed for so doing.

Yet for all that he roused himself the next morning sufficiently to go into town; he cashed a cheque, and with the money he went into an exchange bureau, and bought many dirty hundred franc notes, which he put into a registered envelope and despatched it to Rouen.

It was in this fashion that the old atmosphere re-developed at 53 Malcolm Road. It grew slowly, and the young friendship died hard, but the one grew and the other died, inevitably, infallibly. And the passionate love that Annie bore to Marble, the love that he had roused, was beaten down and trampled underfoot. Passion she had known before, in a vague sort of way, when they had first been married, and love she had always borne him, but the new love, this splendid brilliant thing that had just come into her life, borne of trouble shared with him, and which for this space had illuminated her whole being, was changed to poison and bitterness. It was bad for both of them.

The effect was not yet well marked by the time Easter came, bringing back Winnie from school. She had changed, just as she had changed during the other two terms. She was taller—she nearly overtopped her father now—and she was more beautiful than ever. Her manner had changed, too. She had gained in assurance—it might be better put as insolence—and her voice had gained in its marked throaty quality. Her complexion was wonderful and her figure was marvellous. Her upper lip was short and her eyelids drooping, and she carried herself with an easy erectness that accentuated the arrogance of her manner.

She was head girl of the school now, thanks to a capacity for producing good results in examinations without doing much work beforehand, and thanks also to an unexpected flair for lacrosse and for tennis; she was not the sort of girl to stand any nonsense from old-fashioned parents, not by a long chalk.

At first things did not go too badly. Matters had not declined very much from the old standard of perfection that they had reached during the good time that had just ended. Winnie's drooping lids lifted a trifle in surprise the first lunchtime, when she saw the spotless white cloth and the bright silver, and was given a lunch not very inferior either in quality or quantity to that she was given at school.

But the brief spell of intimacy her parents had enjoyed had left an unfortunate legacy behind it. They could quarrel now, which was more than they had been able to do before, and they rather took advantage of it. The disappointment of the decline of their happiness rasped their nerves, and they displayed a distressing tendency to snap at one another which Winnie deprecated. It was rank bad form for husband and wife to quarrel in public. Winnie considered that her presence was sufficient to make the quarrels take place 'in public'.

Behind the wrinkle in Winnie's brow many things were slowly developing. She liked to think of herself as cold-blooded and calculating. Calculating she may have been; cold-blooded she certainly was not. She could weigh up chances, and make a plan of campaign, but she never chose the cautious plan indicated by those chances. Winnie's cold-bloodedness amounted to an ability to see the folly of recklessness combined with an inability to avoid being reckless.

First of all she was cautious. She refitted her wardrobe to the fullest extent she could possibly contrive; her father paid the bills without a murmur. He still could take delight in the fact that his daughter was at school with two Honourables—daughters of a profiteering war peer—and that during the last holidays she had met several other titled people to speak to. He did not object in the least to paying for her clothes under these circumstances.

Even while Winnie was studying spring fashions she found herself smiling wryly with relief that her parents had this queer fad for living in a poky house in a poky suburb. If they had launched out a bit when they had made their money, as once she had wanted them to, there would not be all this loose cash to throw about. Twelve hundred a year was not much; if they had a big house and a motor-car her father would certainly not be able to pay three hundred a year for her school expenses, nor these big sums for her clothes, and as for the cheque she had just wheedled out of him—well, he would have thought more than twice about giving her that!

Winnie was acutely aware of the atmosphere of insecurity that hung like a fog about 53 Malcolm Road; of its true cause she was, of course, ignorant, but she appreciated it sufficiently to do her best to make hay while the sun still shone. She had plenty of clothes, and she had a monstrous sum in her handbag—an amount undreamed of by her schoolfellows and most certainly unknown to her schoolmistresses. For all the fact that it was a school for profiteers' daughters there would have been a huge commotion if it had got about that Winnie Marble habitually carried over a hundred pounds, a bulky roll of five and ten-pound notes with her. But Winnie was cautious so far; she took pains that it did *not* get about. Money was always useful; and at the back of Winnie's mind there was a half-formed plan, in carrying out which she would find it more than useful, she expected.

Last holiday had been most successful. The girl she had stayed with had, of course, been only a girl, and the other guests who came at odd intervals had hardly noticed her. But they noticed Winnie all right. It would have been hard not to. Winnie, to the annoyance of her hostess and the chagrin of the daughter of the house, had climbed into the position of full guest; she attained brevet woman's rank and clung to it like a leech. The other women had turned up their noses; the men had grinned and played up to her. And two of the men were likely to be useful to Winnie if ever she decided to act on that half-formed plan. They were powers in the world of musical comedy—maybe because they, too, were war profiteers. But for all that it was a little inconvenient that she was not to be asked to that house again. She would be glad to have somewhere to go this holiday.

If she had, the storm might perhaps have been averted; perhaps everything might have been different. As it was, the eventual catastrophe was impossible to avoid.

It began in quite a small way, the way these things do.

'Oh, mother,' said Winnie, 'you're never going out in that hat?'

'Why not?' asked Mrs Marble. She had never liked the way Winnie had dismissed, with a bare word, all the fine clothes she had been buying.

'It's too awful for words. That red and that blue——'

It was unfortunate that she should have said that. The hat was one whose trimming Mrs Marble had altered herself, and she was proud of the result.

'I think it's very nice,' said Mrs Marble.

'Oh, it's not, mother. Those colours swear at each other most frightfully. Oh, dear, and·your coat's all wrinkled at the back. Why don't you learn to put your clothes on properly?'

'I *do* put them on properly. I put them on better than you do. *I* don't look fast.'

The last words slipped out almost without Mrs Marble being aware of them. She felt sore and irritable, and it had been a tradition in her family when she was a little girl that everyone who had the self-assured manner and polished appearance that Winnie affected was 'fast'.

Winnie did not mind being called fast by her mother. She only deigned to reply with a rather unladylike snort. But the word attracted her father's attention, and he looked up sharply. He was irritable, too.

'Don't talk to your mother like that, Winnie,' he said.

'Don't interfere,' snapped Winnie.

She gave a last wrench at the wrinkled coat; but she was cross, and the coat was a hopeless misfit, anyway. Mrs Marble staggered at the wrench. Winnie had meant nothing by it, but it brought Mr Marble to his feet.

'Be careful, my girl,' he said.

It was that 'my girl' which settled the matter. It was a horridly vulgar expression, and it took Winnie straight back to those dark days before she had ever gone to school in Berkshire. She turned and looked at her father, looked him up and down, and as she could find nothing to say she did something far more effective than any speech would have been. She turned away without a word spoken, her upper lip a little curled—not much, that was the annoying part; it implied that her father was not worth being *too* contemptuous about—and her best young ladyish expression on her face. It was more than flesh and blood could stand, especially flesh and blood that had been moistened by just not enough whisky for the last few days.

Marble caught her by the shoulder and swung her round again.

'One word from you, my girl,' he said, 'and you'll be sorry. You're not grown up yet, you know.'

'Aren't I?' said Winnie, 'Aren't I? I'll show you that I am in a minute, if you're not careful. Bh!' she added, manners clean forgotten, 'you and your silly old house, and your silly old furniture, and your silly old clothes. Just look at you both.'

She looked them up and down again, both of them, this time. It was here that Mrs Marble should have played the peacemaker. It was her last opportunity, and she might have flung herself between her husband and her daughter. But she was too cross; partly because she knew that Winnie's sneer at the furniture would have hit her husband in a tender spot.

'Oh, you wicked girl,' she said. 'How dare you speak to us like that? You ought to be grateful to us for all we've done for you.'

Winnie could think of nothing better to say than 'Ought I?' but it was quite enough for her to say. It was the manner, and not the matter, that told. Winnie was too superior altogether, and that throaty accent of hers irritated her parents past all bearing. It reminded her father too painfully of the days when he had been a slave in a bank, and it forced home upon her mother the knowledge that her criticism of her clothes had been sincere, and it gave her an uncomfortable feeling that Winnie knew what she was talking about. It was Mrs Marble that found speech first.

'Yes, you did ought,' she said. 'You owe us the clothes on your back, and all that fine schooling you've had, and —and everything else. So there!'

Winnie had lost her temper thoroughly by now.

'I do, do I?' she said. 'Well, I shan't owe you anything else, so there! I'll go away now, this minute, if you're not careful. I will, I tell you.'

She may have thought that this threat would be sure of silencing them, and making them sorry for what they had said; but she had left out of her reckoning the temper they were in, and the fact that they might not take her literally. Nor was she to know that there was one member in the house who might not be too sorry if she were to carry out her threat—someone who found it very worrying to have to guard his own backyard from his own daughter.

'Poo!' said Mr Marble.

'I will, I tell you. I will. Oh——' And then Winnie stamped her foot at them as they stood there and turned and fled upstairs to her own room. Downstairs they heard the key turn in the lock.

'Oh dear, oh dear,' said Mrs Marble, now that it was over. 'I'll go up to her, shall I?'

'No,' said Marble, 'she's only gone to have a good cry. Didn't you hear her lock her door?'

But Winnie was not having a good cry. She had made her decision in red-hot mood, with a precipitation after her calm deliberation that was characteristic of her. She dragged out her trunks from under her bed and began to pile her clothes into them feverishly. It was all done before she had time to think.

Then she washed her face in cold water and re-powdered carefully. Now that her mind was made up there was nothing that could change it. She put on her hat, her very nicest hat, before the mirror, and walked downstairs again. Before her mother could come out into the hall to make her peace she had gone out, with the front door slamming behind her.

'Gone for a walk,' was Marble's terse explanation when his wife tearfully reported this to him. 'Gone for a walk to get over it. She'll come back soon as right as rain.'

She was back sooner than they expected, however, and she came back in a cab. They heard her key in the door, and a moment afterwards they heard her directing the cab-driver upstairs to where her trunks lay. As the true import of this came home to her Mrs Marble hurried into the hall, wringing her hands.

'Winnie, Winnie,' she wailed. 'We didn't mean it, really we didn't. Winnie, dear, don't go like this. Will, tell her she mustn't.'

But Mr Marble was silent. Winnie had come into the sitting-room to them, defiance in her eyes. They could hear the laboured steps of the cab-driver bringing down the first trunk.

'Will, tell her she mustn't,' said Mrs Marble again.

But Mr Marble still said nothing. He was drumming with his fingers upon the arm of his chair. He was thinking, as hard as his confused mind and the tumult of his thoughts would allow. There was absolutely no denying the fact that it would be more convenient to have Winnie out of the house. One never knew, never. All the books said that it was the little things that gave one away, and the fewer people there were about to notice such things the better. Perhaps Mr Marble would not have considered this in connexion with Winnie, but during that quarrel there was something that forced it upon him. Once more it was that dread family likeness. Winnie had looked rather like John, that time when he had come blundering into the sitting-room; and she had looked rather like young Medland, too. It had shaken him badly.

The heavy steps of the cab-driver were heard redescending the stairs. They paused outside the door, and he coughed apologetically.

'Two trunks and a 'atbox, mum. Is that right?'

'Quite right,' said Winnie, in her throatiest, most musical voice.

And still Mr Marble said nothing.

'Good-bye,' said Winnie. The throatiness disappeared like magic; there was a little break in her voice. It would have taken very little to have diverted her from her purpose.

Mrs Marble looked at her husband; waited for him to speak. All she could do was to wring her hands and choke in her breathing. Still Mr Marble did not speak. Winnie could bear it no longer. She swung round on her heel and ran out of the room, down the hall and out to the waiting cab.

'Charing Cross,' she said to the driver, huskily.

Mrs Marble only reached the gate when they were fifty yards away—beyond recall.

It was all very stupid and silly, and afterwards it seemed as if it might have been avoided—but it really might not.

CHAPTER XV

AND now began the darkest period in all Annie Marble's unhappy life, the last few weeks before its unhappy end. The shadows had massed about 53 Malcolm Road, and as they clustered round ready for the last act of the tragedy poor Annie grew more and more conscious of their presence.

Winnie was gone; of that they could be sure now. They had waited a week in suspense; then they had begun to advertise for her. Discreet little advertisements in the personal columns of the papers—'Winnie. Come back to 53. Everything forgiven. Father and Mother.' That was the most they could do. For a brief half-second while they had been debating what to do there had arisen a hint that they might call in the police, but it vanished at once like a breath of cold air, leaving them looking dumbly at each other without meeting each other's eyes.

Poor Annie spent anxious hours wondering what had

happened to her daughter. There was only one thing that she thought possible, and that was that she was leading 'a life of shame' with one or other of the finely-dressed men she knew. At this late period Annie remembered the flocks of men who had hovered—and more than hovered—about them during those days at the Grand Pavilion Hotel. She was sure that it was this that had happened. Neither she nor her husband knew that Winnie had had all that money with her when she left; nor, thinking the worst as they inevitably did, did they give her credit for her coolness of head that she could summon to her aid if necessary. Annie Marble thought she had driven her daughter into prostitution. It was the bitterest drop she had to swallow.

It was spring, and drifting through the air came the plague. Perhaps it was the self-same plague that had swept across England during the last years of the reign of Edward III; certainly the same plague that had killed its thousands in war-torn France in 1814, and claimed the life of an empress; the same plague that had decimated Europe the last spring of the war, taking more victims than had the war itself; the same plague that, sometimes virulent, sometimes almost negligible, had shown itself every spring since. The disease at which some people still scoff, but which is, nevertheless, deadly: influenza.

It was in the air, and seeking victims. Those who troubled too little about their health; those who were for the moment out of sorts; those who were depressed, or worn with anxiety—they were the victims the plague sought.

And Annie Marble was depressed and worn with anxiety. She was fretting about Winnie, and this was the last straw added to the intolerable burden under which she laboured. Will had returned almost entirely to his old ways; once again he passed his time in the sitting-room, peering drearily through the windows into the backyard. The whisky bottle was continually at his side; the words he had for his wife grew fewer and fewer. Sometimes he could still rouse himself sufficiently to pay her a little attention, and bring a flash of sunshine into her life, but the occasions were rare. Poor Annie!

Then one morning Annie was not well. She had a headache, and she was thirsty. At first she was able to let it pass unheeded; it would go away during the morning, she thought, or at least it would be gone by to-morrow. So she began her day's work, but when it was half completed she felt that she had to sit and rest for a space. The rest seemed to do her good, and she thought to complete the cure by going out to do her shopping. She put on her coat and hat, but even as she went downstairs dizziness came over her and she was forced to acknowledge herself beaten. With an effort of will she went into the sitting-room, where her husband was staring gloomily through the panes.

'Will,' she said, collapsing into a chair, 'I don't feel very well.'

That roused her husband a little, to ask what he could do, and what was the matter. It ended in Mr Marble going forth to do the shopping, leaving her to rest. It was tacitly understood between them, before he left her, that she was to rest in the sitting-room, whence she could keep an eye through the windows.

And the next day Annie felt worse than ever. But even in her illness she found something to comfort her. Marble was a little alarmed, and he showed it in the concern he evinced about her. He asked how she was very gently, and he tried to minister to her in a clumsy man's fashion. Poor Annie was quite fluttered and pleased, despite her sickness, by the attention he paid her. As he guided her to a chair and propped her back with cushions where it hurt, and asked what else he could do, she was almost glad she was ill. For she had refused to stay in bed. That was like her. If she could stand, she would get out of bed. And she could not only stand, but she could walk, when her dizziness permitted it. She was in a high fever, but to that she did not pay much attention. But she agreed, nevertheless, that it might perhaps be advisable that Will should do the shopping that day. He even volunteered that he should, and sallied out, shopping basket in hand, and a little list of things that were needed. He had forgotten one or two items the day before.

While he was gone, Annie sat in the drawing-room. Her mouth was dry, and there was an unpleasant taste in it, and her head felt queer, and there was a strange sort of doubtfulness about things when she looked at them. There were pains in her body and joints, too. But, for all that, she still felt the joy of her husband's loving attention.

But Will had hardly gone when the postman dropped a letter through the door with his double knock. It was the eleven o'clock postman—he who brought the continental mail. Annie walked weakly to the door and picked up the letter, and went back weakly to the drawing-room. Not until she had sat down did she look at the envelope—she was not sure enough of her legs to read it standing up. But she was very interested as to what it might be. For perhaps it might be news of Winnie.

The envelope was addressed most queerly. The writing was large and sprawling. The first letter of the address was a big 'A'. The second was an 'M'. The third was a 'W'. The letter was obviously from foreign parts, for the address ended 'Angleterre' and Annie knew that meant 'England' in a foreign tongue. Thus——

> *A. M. W. Marble,*
> *53 Malcolm Road,*
> *Dulwich,*
> *Londres,*
> *Angleterre.*

Annie looked at the envelope a long time. Clearly the 'A' and the 'M' referred to her—was she not Ann Mary Marble? The 'W' and the absence of any 'Mrs' bothered her. But it might be usual in letters from abroad to leave out the 'Mrs' and being from abroad it might contain news about Winnie just as much as if it had been posted in England. Annie opened it, and took out the letter. It took several seconds for the import of the first few words to pierce home to her, but as soon as she had grasped their meaning she sank back half fainting in her chair. The letter was in English, and it began 'My dearest, darling Will'.

Recovering herself, Annie read the remainder of the letter. She could not understand some of it—the cruel satire of it was beyond her, dulled as her mind was by her fever, and what she did understand left her heartbroken. All through the letter the writer addressed Will in terms of the most flamboyant affection; it made some reference which she did not understand to her, Annie, and it ended by asking for money—'The same as you sent me before, darling'.

Annie sat still, the letter crumpled up in her hand. There was no address on the letter, and the signature was rather illegible and consisted of a French word. But she knew from whom the letter came. It might have been instinct, or it might have been recognition of the style, but she knew. The tears which might have helped her were denied her by the fever. All she could do was to sit and think distortedly over everything. So Will did not love her, after all her dreams and hopes. Instead, he was writing to this Frenchwoman, and sending her money. All this tenderness of his, and the passion he had shown a little while back—just after *she* had gone, Annie realized with a sob in her throat—were mere pretences. With strange prescience she guessed that it was to keep her in a good temper when he found that she knew about his secret. A half-formed resolution rose in the maelstrom of her thoughts that she would betray him at the first opportunity, but she put it aside unconsidered. She loved him too much. Her heart was broken, and she was very, very unhappy.

She sat there alone, for what seemed like hours.

Later came Marble, but she roused herself at the sound of the key in the door sufficiently to thrust the letter into the bosom of her dress, and when he came to ask how she was she managed to gasp out 'I think I'm ill. Oh——' Then she fell forward in the chair. She *was* ill, very ill. Marble helped her up to bed, to the big gilt bed where the cupids climbed eternally, with its lavish canopy-rail and bulging ornament. But when she had recovered sufficiently to undress she thrust the letter into her little private drawer before calling to him in her cracked, fevered voice for his help.

Next day she was worse. Marble bent over her anxiously as she lay there in the gaudy bed. She tossed about, from side to side, and she hardly knew him. There were only those two in the house, and he was worried. Worried to death. Of sick nursing he knew nothing. There was not even a clinical thermometer in the house. If she were to die—! But he refused to consider her dying. There would be one fewer in the secret, it is true, but the disadvantages would be overwhelming. And there would be questions asked if she were to die without receiving medical attention. Come what might, he must fetch a doctor. He must bring a stranger into his house, the house that he guarded so urgently. There was no help for it, no help for it at all. He saw that she had all his intelligence could suggest that she might want, and then slipped away quietly downstairs and out to where the nearest brass plate hung at a gate. A white-capped maid-servant took his message and told him that the doctor would be round shortly.

Dr Atkinson was a thin rat of a man, with sandy hair and eyebrows, neither young nor old, with a keen glance behind his pince-nez. He felt her pulse, took her temperature; he noticed her troubled breathing and the way she tossed and turned in the bed. She was nearly delirious; indeed, her speech was confused, and twice she muttered something that he just did not catch. He turned and looked keenly at Marble.

'Who's looking after her?' he asked.

'I am,' said Marble—a trifle sullenly, Atkinson thought, later.

'Are you alone?'

'Yes. My daughter's—away at present.'

'Well, you'd better get somebody in. Some neighbour or somebody. She'll need careful attention if we're to avoid pneumonia.'

Marble looked at him blankly. Get somebody in? Have someone else in the house, poking and prying about? And Annie, there, nearly delirious! Marble had caught a word or two of what she had muttered, of what Atkinson had not heard, and it set him trembling.

Atkinson was looking round the room, with its queer furnishing of gilt. He was trying to estimate the income of this man who apparently did not go to work.

'What about a nurse?' he said. 'I'll send one in, shall I?'

Marble found his tongue.

'No,' he said, with overmuch vehemence—he was sadly overtried. 'I won't have a nurse. I can do all the nursing myself. I won't have a nurse.'

Atkinson shrugged his shoulders.

'Well, if you won't, you won't. But she'll need very careful nursing, I tell you that. You must——' he went on to outline all that Marble must do. But all the time he was debating within himself over this strange man who lived alone with his wife in a poky house furnished like Buckingham Palace, whose daughter was—away, at present, who did no work, and who was violently opposed to having anyone nurse his wife.

And Marble guessed at his curiosity, and cursed at it within himself, with the sweat running cold under his clothes.

'Right, I'll look in again this afternoon,' said Atkinson.

He did. He looked in again twice a day during all the next week.

And during that week Marble fretted and wore himself to pieces under the burden of his troubles. Everything was madly worrying. Atkinson alone, with his sharp eyes everywhere, was enough to madden him, yet to add to it all the great worry of his life returned to him and nagged at him more than ever he had known it before. Marble found his harassed mind returning continually to work out hateful possibilities; whether or no Atkinson might find something out; whether he had heard anything of what Annie was continually muttering; what the neighbours, as well as Atkinson, thought of his refusing to call in the assistance of anyone else. He knew that they were all interested in what went on in his house, he knew how they sneered enviously at all his fine possessions, and at Annie's clothes and Winnie's grand manner—and they were probably burningly interested in what had happened to Winnie, though by good luck they might think she was still at school.

Annie herself worried him, too. She was a 'difficult' patient. She would hardly speak to him, and would turn from him in horror on those occasions when she was most nearly delirious. She needed a great deal of attention. Marble had to struggle to do invalid cookery for her—he, who had never so much as touched a saucepan in his life. He had to do it well, too, for that brute Atkinson was continually coming in, and more than once he demanded to see and taste the concoctions he had prepared for her. Marble struggled along with Mrs

Beeton, the same Mrs Beeton as Annie had lingered over for his sake, and attended to the tradesmen who once more came calling—Marble had to allow that; Atkinson was too sharp for him to attempt to do the shopping and leave his patient. Rushing from the kitchen to the door, and from the door to the bedroom, whenever Annie rang the handbell that stood by the bed, and from the bedroom back to the kitchen, Marble wore himself out. It was rare that even two attempts brought success to his unskilful cookery; he seemed to be cooking all the time.

And as a crowning worry came the fear that he would be taken ill, too. In that case Atkinson, the interfering busybody, would step in and have them taken away to hospital. If he were delirious like Annie! He shuddered at the thought. So it was wildly necessary that he should retain his health. Marble had never worried about his health before, but now he paid for it in full. He took his temperature every few minutes, he studied his body attentively, and he stopped drinking the whisky for which his nerves shrieked.

The strain told on him. The worrying days and the broken nights—for he had to attend to Annie frequently during the nights—broke his already strained nerves to pieces. And he could not forget about the garden. That was continuously in his thoughts, too. If anything, it was worse now. Marble found himself, whenever the jangle of Annie's bell roused him out of his sleep, and after he had done what she wanted, creeping downstairs to peer out into the dark garden to see that all was secure. He even began to wake on his own during the night and go down, and he had never done that before.

Strange to tell, Annie recovered. It was more really than Atkinson expected, and it seems stranger still when it is remembered that she did not want to recover. For she did not. Annie wanted to die.

But she recovered. The fever left her, very thin, very

pale, with the shining pallor of the invalid, and she was able to leave off the pneumonia jacket that Marble had hurriedly contrived, and sit up in bed dressed in one of her opulent, overlaced nightdresses and a dressing-jacket and boudoir cap. Atkinson told Marble that she was not yet quite out of danger. There was always a risk after a bad attack of influenza. There might be grave heart trouble, or even now pneumonia might intervene if she were to get up too soon.

'But, of course,' said Atkinson, 'there's not much chance of her getting up for a bit yet. She's too weak to stand at present.'

Annie lay in bed, thinking. She was thinking with the clearness of thought, harsh and raw as a winter's morning, that comes after a period of high fever. Over her brooded the dreadful depression following influenza, the poison-ous depression which darkens the most hopeful outlook. And Annie's outlook was anything but hopeful. Down-stairs she could hear her husband moving about on one of his endless household tasks, and her lips writhed at the thought of him. She did not hate him, she could not hate him, even now. But she felt she hated herself. And she had lost her husband's love, the love which for a brief space had made the whole world seem a wonderful place. Looking ahead, as far as she was able to look ahead, she could see nothing to hope for. She was tor-mented by the hideous knowledge of what lay in the barren flower-bed in the backyard; the whole future held out no promise for her. She would have faced the peril that hung over her husband—and over herself as well, she realized—gladly, had she only been sure that her husband wished her to do so. But instead she was only sure of the opposite. He would be glad to have her out of the way, and she——? She would be glad to be out of the way.

That set her thoughts moving swiftly on another tack.

It might be easy enough. But if only she had died during this illness! She tried to piece together in her mind what that book of Will's had said about the stuff—that—that —the stuff that still stood on the locked shelves in the bathroom. Death is practically instantaneous. Death is practically instantaneous.

That meant an easy death, a quick death. There would be no trouble about it, none at all. Oh, it would be the best way. That clearness of thought was in evidence at present. Will was downstairs, and he was unlikely to disturb her for some time. It could be done, and better do it now, and save trouble, save trouble.

Annie threw off the bedclothes and set her feet to the floor. Even as she did so she found how unsteady she was. The room seemed to swing round her in a great arc; she nearly fell to the floor, and she would have done had she not, by a vast effort, seized the bed and collapsed across it. It took several minutes for her to recover. She tried again, more tentatively, and again she had hard work to save herself from falling. She could not walk, that was certain. But that would not prevent her.

Slowly, with infinite precaution, she lowered herself to the floor. Then she crawled across the floor towards the window. It was dreadfully hard work; she could only move slowly. The cold air and the coldness of the linoleum bit deep into her, and she shuddered as she moved.

She reached the chest of drawers, and clutching the knobs she pulled herself to her feet, standing there swaying. It took several seconds for her to grow used to this position. Once she swayed dangerously, but her grip on the drawer-knobs saved her. Then she pulled open one of the drawers and did what she had been wanting to do all through her illness. She pulled out the strange letter, and read it through, as closely as her swimming eyes would allow. She was right. There was no hope for her in it. It began 'My dearest, darling Will' sure enough. Once again the satire was lost on her. She reeled as she stood. Then she thrust the letter back into the drawer and closed it.

Somehow she was still able to think clearly. The next thing she wanted was the key. All Will's keys were on a ring on the dressing-table. She had to crawl there to get them. Then she crawled—oh, so slowly—out through the door to the bathroom. The effort of standing up again when she reached the shelves was almost too much for her, but she achieved it. She stood listening for a brief space, just to make sure that Will was still busy downstairs. It would never do for him to come up now and find her there. But it was all quiet. She could just hear him, pottering about in the kitchen. The key fitted easily, and she opened the glass door. There on the shelf, just as she had seen it so long ago, stood the bottle— potassium cyanide. She took it in her hand, fondled it, she almost smiled as she looked at it.

On the edge of the bath stood one of her medicine glasses. She filled it half full, the neck of the bottle chattering on the rim of the glass, and replaced the bottle. As it stood there on the shelf she tried to bow to it; she tried to say 'thank you' to it. And she locked the shelf door again tidily.

She stood hesitating for a space, holding on to the edge of the bath. She did not want to die here, in this cold place. She would much rather die in her splendid great bed with the cupids twined about it. It would be risky trying to get back, but she thought she would run the risk. Oh, but it was so hard. She crawled along the floor, pushing the medicine glass in front of her, the keys trailing by their ring from one finger. Very hard it was, but she succeeded in the end. She hardly spilt a drop on the way.

The medicine glass stood on the floor beside the bed.

It was as much as she could manage to pull herself half erect and fall across the bed. She had to lie and rest again, after that. But now at last she was ready. She must make everything neat and tidy first. With fumbling fingers she drew the bedclothes round her, and set her boudoir cap straight and settled the lace at her throat. Then she leaned over the side of the bed and took the glass in her hand. There was no hesitation in her raising it to her lips. She drained it, and the glass fell from her fingers to the floor and rolled under the bed.

But even now things went hardly for her. That cyanide had been kept in solution for over a year, slowly reacting with itself and with the atmosphere. It was not an easy death, not a quick death.

CHAPTER XVI

MR MARBLE had just finished his preliminary morning's work when Dr Atkinson's rat-tat-tat came at the door.

'How is she this morning?' asked Atkinson as they went up the stairs together.

'She seemed a little bit down when I was with her last. But I haven't been up to her for some time,' said Marble.

They entered the room, where Annie lay in the big gilt bed, with the other gilt furniture blazing about her. She lay there in a natural attitude, and there was a trace of colour in her cheeks. But there was something different, which flashed to Atkinson's trained eye the moment it rested on her.

'She's dead!' said Atkinson, moving forward.

Marble was there before him, standing by the bed with his hands clasped in front of him. It is impossible to say whether he was moved or not; all that he was conscious of at the moment was that his heart was thumping and thudding within him the way it always did nowadays when anything unusual happened. It beat and it beat, and his hands shook with the vibrations.

'Her heart, I suppose,' said Atkinson, coming to the bedside.

He might have spared Marble the technical details if only Marble had appeared upset. But Marble did not. He was too busy thinking—his mind had started racing away as it always did, to the accompaniment of the thudding of his heart. He was working out all the details of how this change would affect him; what difference it would make to his chances of continuing to avoid detection. All he could do was to stare at the body while his hands shook and his face remained stolid. Clearly his thoughts were far away.

With an effort he recalled himself. Suspicion, suspicion! He must do all he could to avoid suspicion. He looked sidelong at Atkinson, and caught Atkinson looking sidelong at him. He started, and tried to appear concerned.

Now up to that moment Atkinson had not had the least trace of suspicion, but that glance and that start set thoughts flooding into his mind. He bent over the body, and noticed something else, something which roused him to the highest pitch of suspicion.

'I must make a slight examination,' he said, 'could you go downstairs and get me—get me a spoon? A silver spoon.'

Marble went without a word, like an ox to the slaughter. No sooner had he left the room than Atkinson sprang into activity. He tiptoed across to see that **Marble** was really gone, and then he hurried back. There was a trace of foam on the dead woman's lips. There was a trace of a faint odour. He glanced under the bed; a medicine glass lay there. He picked it up and looked at it. A little of the contents remained. Close examination of this made him certain. When Marble came back to the room he was scribbling something on a sheet from his pocket-book.

'I shall want this as well,' he said. 'Will you go and give this note to the boy in my car outside, and ask him to go straight home for it?'

Marble took it. The note was an order to the boy to fetch a policeman, but Marble did not know that.

So they hanged William Marble for the murder of his wife. It was a simple case. They proved that she had died of cyanide poisoning, and they proved that Marble had cyanide in his possession. Dr Atkinson swore that Annie Marble would be quite incapable of going into the bathroom to get it for herself. Everything else pointed towards the same end. He would not have a nurse for her, but had insisted on doing everything himself, against the urgent advice of his doctor. Neighbours came flocking in, eager to swear that there had been bad blood between Marble and his wife for a long time, and that they had often heard quarrels and cries. They even found downstairs a number of books on crime, and in one book on medical jurisprudence the page where cyanide poisoning was discussed was much thumbed and dirty, through constant study. And for a motive—well, they found in a drawer a letter from a woman that amply proved a motive. It was a letter that Marble knew nothing about, but no one believed him when he said so. In fact, Marble went down through history as an extraordinarily clumsy murderer.

And Winnie inherited twelve hundred a year.